...writing that is so beautiful it takes your breath away, sharp as a knife, whose short, polished phrases shine with a cold brilliance; writing like the February dawn at the start of the book: "enough to freeze the blood".

Le Monde diplomatique

Through their alternating voices, full of rage, anger, unsatisfied desires, Yanick Lahens' fine, precise, poetic and sensual writing depicts the destiny of an ordinary family. She forcefully evokes the breakdown of a country where hope nevertheless begins to stir: the hope of dignity redisovered.

Le Monde des livres

A novel that is at times musical, with glints of a language full of vivid images, at other times more raw – sex and death, with no frills – which brings to light a certain reality of Haiti. A story that will leave its mark on the memory.

Psychologies

The Colour of Dawn

The Colour of Dawn

Yanick Lahens

Translated by
Alison Layland

SEREN
DISCOVERIES

Seren is the book imprint of
Poetry Wales Press Ltd
Nolton Street, Bridgend, Wales

www.serenbooks.com
facebook.com/SerenBooks
Twitter: @SerenBooks

Original French text © Yanick Lahens, 2008
Translation © Alison Layland, 2013

First published in French as *La Couleur de l'Aube* by Éditions Sabine
Wespieser in 2008

This translation is published with the support of the Centre National
du Livre

The right of Yanick Lahens to be identified
as the Author of this Work has been asserted
in accordance with the Copyright, Designs
and Patents Act, 1988.

ISBN 978-1-78172-057-8
Mobi: 978-1-78172-058-5
Epub: 978-1-78172-059-2

A CIP record for this title is available from
the British Library

Cover image: Getty Images

The publisher works with the financial assistance
of the Welsh Books Council

Printed by CPI Group (UK) Ltd, Croydon, CR0 4YY

The Colour of Dawn

...for in their secret awareness of Him, He was not the God of three faces they sang about. They knew quite well that he had four, and that the fourth explained Sula. They had lived with various forms of evil all their days, and it wasn't that they believed God would take care of them. It was rather that they knew God had a brother and that brother hadn't spared God's son, so why should he spare them?

Toni Morrison
Sula

Oh, how can you expect me to put
all these words into a letter
– eyewitness of a time
that has not come to its last meal
of cannibals?

Georges Castera
Lettre d'octobre

ONE

Stealing a march on the dawn, I have opened the door onto the night. Not without first going down on my knees and praying to God – how could I not pray to God on this island, where the Devil has such a hold and must be rubbing his hands in glee? In this house, where he has stealthily established himself as each day passes.

Three times in succession I have recited a psalm of David, taking care to emphasise each syllable so that, in speaking so intensely to God, I am doing something that counts, ensuring that the sky above my head is more than an empty half-gourd:

> *When the wicked advance against me*
> *To devour my flesh...*

All night my eyes peered into the shadows. All night my ears strained to hear the crackling of gunfire in the distance – something you always want to imagine distant, very distant. Until that day when death comes, bleeding, to our door. Until the day it spatters our walls. Like the others, all the others, I am waiting.

Fignolé, my younger brother, didn't come home last night. I didn't hear him carefully opening the front door, nor noisily relieving himself in the backyard, as he so often does. And his bed, which serves by day as a couch in the living room, is untouched. For several months now I have been worried about Fignolé. I'm not the only one. How could anyone not worry about Fignolé? Fignolé, who has always held our lives on a string to the point of strangulation, whom fear has not yet succeeded in bringing to his knees. Where could he have spent the night? Where...?

It's precisely half past four... This moment, between darkness and light, is my favourite time. The time when my thoughts can turn freely to those who occupy this house, to all those whose whereabouts are lost to me, or who are too far away. The hour of my accumulated resentments, the hour of my numerous hatreds, my expectations ranged before me, my hardships that are enough to make me cry with rage. Resentments, hatreds, hardships – I will soon have gathered them all, without exception, like a gaggle of chattering gossips. I carry inside myself so many other women, strangers who dog my footsteps, who live in my shadow, restless in my skin. Not one of them will be deaf to the call of this young woman, not yet thirty, on whom time has left its mark. A young woman struck down some years ago who pretends to carry on living as if nothing had happened.

Ti Louze has already gone to fetch water from the neighbourhood fountain. She has tucked away in a corner the rush mat she lays out as a bed, right by the door to the backyard, together with the rags she piles up to sleep under every night. Let's hope she will return unscathed from those inevitable riots around the water, where we learn to cut our teeth, sharpen our fangs, at a very early stage. We are devoured by rage like dogs. Soon we will grow tails, walk the ground on four paws. It's only a matter of time.

God, it's cold! I put the coffee pot on the gas stove in the backyard and carefully raise the collar of my bathrobe that was once red but has long since faded to an indistinct brownish colour. The channel that runs along the far wall of this tiny courtyard gives off a persistent stench of decay and urine. It was wreathed in indistinct wisps when I opened the door. And to cap it all, Fignolé has not come home. One of us should help Ti Louze to carry the rubbish to the foul-smelling corner where all the neighbourhood's residents pile up their garbage again and again without any hope of the public services coming to collect it.

The February dawn is enough to freeze the blood. Wedged into the rocking chair, arms folded over my chest, legs stretched open in front of me, I reign over this backyard as if it were a great palace of solitude where I can allow myself a few moments of madness. A mad queen, my body in turmoil, shaken from the tips of my toes to the roots of my hair! I can still believe my body has a purpose. Look, there beneath my left breast, my life beats in secret like a captive bird. I sometimes feel it flutter until it is enough to stifle my breath. Sitting like an abundant cow, I await an attentive hand that knows what to do, to awake it in a noisy beating of wings.

To draw it from its slough of despond.

To help it recover from this futile wearing-down.

I wait...

TWO

My skin has the heady fragrance of orange and custard-apple leaves, generously applied after steeping for hours in a basin in the sun. Behind the metal sheet that serves as our backyard screen, I used the infusion to meticulously wash my face, stomach, arms and legs before sleep caught up with me. I am a woman suffused with a lively glow, my body divested of much of its childish awkwardness, to be replaced with a vigour and suppleness which delight me.

How long have I taken to become a woman? I don't know. My hips have assumed a bold fullness. My thighs have lengthened like palm trees. As the days go by, a deep cosy hollow has formed between my breasts. A fine line between my navel and my pubic hair has darkened and become an object of mystery and desire. When I was still young enough for Mother to wash me, she would often say this line meant my firstborn would be a boy. Now it is a curious detail that arouses men's imagination and their passion, something I have not yet fully explored; something for which the moment of reckoning is still far off, very far off. And then there is Luckson... I only have to close my eyes to see, again and again, his bare chest seeking my breast, his keen eyes close to mine, and I succumb to insolence and desire. Yet I am an ordinary young woman, totally ordinary. I am so well aware of this that, day after day, I work away at transforming this ordinariness into something precious. I love Luckson's slim hips. I love his mouth with its warning, his impudent hands. Luckson – honey and danger.

I open my eyes with a feeling of pleasure simply at existing, next to the sound of Mother breathing in her sleep. With a secret music deep in the hottest, most vital part of me, which soothes my ears, puts a spark in my eyes, animates my hands, burns my lips. Between two bursts of distant gunfire, Mother's sighs kept me awake for part of the night. I don't know what apparitions wandered through her sleep, what visitors ravaged her. Rising from the bed, I take care to keep my movements slight and ensure that I avoid disturbing the arrangement she has placed meticulously on the altar of her spirit Dambala.

Mother would rather go without buying clothes or food than cease honouring her extended family of African spirits, her loas, the Mysteries, the Invisibles, as she calls them. Above all, Dambala, who sits enthroned at the core of her life, who transports her and brings her back like a stalk of straw in the wind. Three or four times a year, she believes she is obliged to pamper them in turn, Dambala first, then Ogou and Erzulie Fréda. Only yesterday she lit a candle to Erzulie Fréda, placing it in the centre of the little altar she has dedicated to her behind the wardrobe. Three pink flamingo flowers have been placed before it, so beautiful you would think they were natural, freshly gathered from a lady's flower garden. Fignolé presented them to Mother when he got his first wage. Mother thinks that Erzulie, a flirt like no other, must have been delighted to see her putting a few drops of her cheap eau de Cologne on a pink satin handkerchief and placing it in a small willow basket. She then took the trouble to satisfy the spirit's huge appetite by serving her three nut slices on a fine porcelain plate, a plate that my employer, Mme Herbruch, left behind in her office one June afternoon and which I stole. Yes, stole. Why June, why that particular afternoon? I couldn't begin to explain. Still, the next day, my eyes impassive and calmly meeting hers, I helped her myself to turn the shop upside-down searching for it.

'That plate means a lot to me, Joyeuse.'

She worked herself up into a temper three days in a row, then never mentioned it again. The anger she expressed over the loss of that plate fascinated me. I remained unmoved inside, the better to observe her and to draw whatever conclusions I could from that range of feelings caused by the loss of something so trifling. Mme Herbruch was, after all, someone who could spare one plate!

Mother's spirits and Angélique's God have drawn a deep line of demarcation between them and me. I have weighed Angélique's respectable God against my Mother's illicit ones and remain unsatisfied. From the far bank where I set out my stakes in the height of noon, blown by fresh winds, I see the two of them fighting with shadows, blind and groping. I have chosen the light, wind and fire – even if they were to strike me blind, even if I had to give up my skin.

I'm in a hurry to go out, to find the fresh breath of the dawn. To leave this house, which seeks to imbue my skin with a musty staleness, the residues of sweat, those signs of deprivation and lack of water, all those clinging smells, the age-old scent of the poor. A house where we are hardly able to breathe in the night. Mother has not lost that annoying habit, from her distant peasant life, of going round before bed and sealing the windows, blocking up the cracks with any bits of fabric that come to hand. All gaps sealed, she keeps the house closed up like a fist, from a fear of all the visible and invisible creatures that await nightfall to come alive. Mother says the night is so favourable to bad air and apparitions!

THREE

A few scattered lights are still shining as night drags its feet. I have switched on the radio, to continue my conversation with God. The journalist-preacher with his shrill, nasal voice has kept his appointment with the Creator and with us: 'Brothers and sisters, open your hearts…'. I hardly hear the first words of his morning prayer before I am back on my feet despite myself, as if a strange force were drawing me towards Fignolé's empty bed. And I take Joyeuse by surprise, her shoulders slumped in stupor, standing before the same bed. She turns as I approach. Immediately I see in her expression that mix of feelings that she believes she can hide from me. As she sees me take several steps towards her, she suddenly changes her attitude, assuming the airs of a grandly-dressed uptown woman. A gesture here, a sigh there, her hands at her throat like a film star. When I remark to her that Fignolé hasn't come home, she does her usual trick of acting as if she knows everything and is not unduly worried about her brother.

'Night must have come down before he realised and he had to sleep at a friend's.'

I don't believe a single word of her reply. Not a word. And nor does she. Carry on, my dear Joyeuse; you carry on taking me for the greatest fool of them all.

Joyeuse, with a backside fit for parading about all the pavements of the city, will soon choose a figure-hugging dress, apply eau de toilette scented with jasmine and ylang-ylang and make up her face with colours to stop passers-by in their tracks. Joyeuse has an unshakeable faith in her lipstick, her breasts and her buttocks.

As for me, Angélique Méracin, I give the impression of wisdom, great wisdom. A sacrificed mother. A submissive daughter. An exemplary sister. Devoted to the sick in a hospital that has nothing. No-one has known me go with a man, either, not one. A woman without appetites, Angélique Méracin continues to serve, to obey, to smile. And so she is full of anger, run through with bad thoughts, shaken by delirious outbursts. And I hate it all. I hate this house. I hate this street, this city, this island.

I listen. Ti Louze is returning from the public fountain. Here she is, barefoot, her plaits coming loose, her dress a little more torn than yesterday and clinging to her skin like seaweed. Bent beneath the weight of two large bottles of water, Ti Louze does not dare meet my eyes. And with good reason! She woke too late and will be hard pushed to make the three trips to the fountain to fill the large plastic tank on the other side of the latrines.

I have taken a few steps towards the bedroom I occupy with Gabriel, my son. Well, I call it a bedroom although it isn't in reality – I have merely put up a makeshift partition between this front room and the backyard to gain some privacy. Needless to say, the house is full to the brim. We can hear each other breathing. And of course, love has taken on the hues of our grudges, has become mixed and confused with our resentments. God obliges us to stay crowded together in all our moods, our resentments and our smells, as a way of putting us to the test, the better to serve Him.

In an hour's time I'll wake Gabriel to get ready for school. His soul nurtured in the splendour of the Scriptures, Gabriel should at this very moment be immersed in biblical dreams, glorious and epic. Sleeping with his hands curled into fists, legs spreadeagled, he can at last enjoy our large bed to himself. Standing on the threshold of my bedroom, I watch him from the corner of my eye, without ceasing to listen out for the sounds coming from the only real bedroom, the one that Mother shares with Joyeuse. Mother turned over a few moments ago, making the bedsprings creak beneath the weight of her bones that are beginning to get old. Her shoulders, I'm sure, will sag a little more in a while, when she realises that Fignolé has not come home. Then she will head slowly for the backyard and silently invoke her gods, her bold loas. Then, to the rhythm of the rocking chair, she will say her rosary, her eyes closed the better to see the other God, the one with the long white beard. You never know exactly which of these two universes is the one Mother moves in.

But at seven o'clock her ear is always glued to the radio; nothing in the world would make her miss the news, nothing. She gets a strange pleasure from listening to these voices that spell out our troubles every day, several times a day. Mother listens to them all: the strident and the clipped, the bass registers and the shrill, the drawling, the sing-song, the casual and the serious. Mother has been through rain, fire and blood. She says that, having lived for sixty years on this island, she is beyond the reach of shadows, beyond the reach of darkness. That her body may not yet exude the smell of a corpse but she is already dead.

And so when the journalist, with an appropriate and familiar voice, announces that an illicit gathering took place yesterday, Sunday, in the city centre, that armed men opened fire on some young people in a suburb to the north of the city, Mother just smiles a strange rictus of a smile, her jaw inflated with too many words, and flicks at the hem of her nightshirt with a swollen, arthritic right hand.

February has touched our daybreaks with cold hands.

The pallid, milky light of the night dissolves into the colours of the horizon. I adjust Mother's shawl. Joyeuse, sitting on her heels, sips her coffee without saying a word – and with good reason. Joyeuse has not been one of us for a long time, not since Uncle Nériscat, Mother's cousin, paid for her to study with the Sisters of Wisdom, in the uptown district.

The three of us are thrown into turmoil by thoughts hard to bear, and I swear that we will avoid speaking openly of Fignolé's absence, despite everything. We are too afraid to do so.

FOUR

Angélique is already outside preparing Gabriel's meal. She often chooses this uncertain hour, away from our scrutiny, to unravel all the knots of kindness, reason and wisdom that hold together this gloomy, remote life of hers. Angélique's life is lived at a low level, barely taking off from the ground. Angélique skims the foam of the days. I can't remember the last time she laughed so the sun danced in her eyes. Truly, I can't remember.

Since Gabriel was born, Angélique's eyes have lost their ability to ensnare. Her body has laid down its arms. She keeps all her happiness tightly bound in a severe bun at the nape of her neck. I have difficulty coming to terms with this new Angélique; I find it hard to let go of the other Angélique who was lively and full of laughter, blazing under the sun. A notion of pure joy, of abstract happiness remains at the sound of her name. How I miss my sister, whose happiness and contagious bliss always went before her, who made me believe that the sun of my childhood would never set, who made every day a delicious flow of honey – despite the days when we went hungry, the days of pretence from just above the bottom end of the scale, the very bottom. We were always prepared to pretend, as if we went to sleep sated, our thirst quenched. As if our clothes were not held together by Mother's ingenuity and mending skills. As if we were not always a hair's breadth away from being expelled from school. As if, indeed, we hadn't sometimes been expelled. As if, as if…

Since my childhood I have been at war. Angélique knew how to make it a happy war. I learned from her the rough, wild strength of that pride. How I miss that Angélique, whom a crafty, boastful man with an 'it's your lookout' attitude stole from me one ordinary day, against a backdrop of sky, earth and sea. This bully in the making must just have raised his head above the surface of our sea of poverty, for I recall he was wearing his shirt open to his navel and his smile revealed a gold incisor. Mother had clearly not had time to give Angélique sufficient warning, to remind her to be wary of strangers lying in wait by the roadside.

Angélique now has a great shadow on her heart. Between the church services and the petty cruelties she bestows on the household, she has no time either to receive the love of God or to give love. Yet Angélique has just one thing on her lips: 'God and His love', 'God and His works', 'God, God, God…'. I even suspect she uses her profession to distance herself from the sufferings of us mortals, and uses prayer to measure the extent to which she can resist earthly pleasures. Her heart is closed and the space between her thighs has been flooded with sadness. The connection is obvious. She knows it as well as I do, but would never admit it, never.

Earlier, when I made to join her outside for coffee, I saw that Fignolé's bed was empty and the sheets had not been disturbed. This fact froze my blood, but I revealed nothing as I heard Angélique open the door to the backyard. She simply said to me:

'Joyeuse, Fignolé didn't come home last night.'

And I replied, 'I know.' Cloaking myself with the air of an eccentric diva that I use when my heart is set to race, I added, 'He must have slept at a friend's place.'

Angélique made no comment, but I know she didn't believe me. For all her devout airs, Angélique is as sharp as an old monkey. When she moved away again towards the backyard, I took the opportunity of having a quick look behind the only cupboard in the living room, where a panel has worked loose. I know this is where Fignolé has taken to slipping the lyrics of the songs he writes, his desire for secrecy inspired by a lingering adolescence with its mysteries, its violence and its games. Without pausing to reflect for a second, I slipped my hand in. I didn't expect to find anything but papers, but my hand met with something cold and metallic. I knew immediately it was a gun.

'What on earth can Fignolé be doing with a gun?'

I drew it out quickly to examine it and convince myself. The barrel, the trigger, the butt. I closed my eyes for a few moments to gain strength to bear the violent music in my blood, which threatened to suffocate me. My hand was shaking.

But I remembered the tale told to me as a child by Mother one evening at nightfall; the tale of a woman who had gained all the strength in the world by swallowing a sacred stone given to her by a mage. Since then I have kept beneath my breast a small imaginary grey stone as a talisman against the evil spells of this island. My thoughts were all on this little grey stone as I tucked the gun beneath my nightshirt together with the few papers that had also been hidden in that cranny. In the bedroom I placed the gun in a box on top of the wardrobe and stowed the papers in my bag next to the bed. Despite all my acrobatics, despite all these comings and goings, Mother didn't notice a thing. Lying beneath the sheets, she simply emitted a lengthy stifled moan as she turned towards me.

I have hardly begun to drink my coffee when Mother joins us in the backyard a few minutes later. She simply says: 'Do either of you know where Fignolé spent the night?' and doesn't wait for a reply. Mother's suffering is obvious. She suffers in silence. Something has been torn from her. She submits totally to this void, this great empty space, submerged in suffering and the waiting for Fignolé, but she won't talk about it. Mother must have faltered by her son's bed and invoked her loas as if grasping a pair of crutches. Mother falters but never falls. While Mother lives, the end of the world will never arrive.

Despite a certain plumpness accumulated with the years, Mother is still beautiful, though it is not that same beauty that was considered a scandal some years ago. Mother is a sovereign in decline, and this morning a tragic sovereign. The waiting turns her mouth into a remote island in the middle of her face, with her eyes like far horizons. Her hands resting on her knees, she murmurs as her whole body sways:

> *Holy Mary, mother of God,*
> *Pray for us, poor sinners…*

She hasn't said a single word about the absence of Fignolé. Not a word. Instead she raises her voice against the whip, the rigoise that Angélique has used on Ti Louze's back and Gabriel's frail legs. I join Mother in this strange chorus and soon we are all three of us yelling. Deep down, we know that Ti Louze and Gabriel are strangers to these cries, to our anger. We yell all the same. We yell because we cannot talk of the only thing that would relieve us, the only thing that would restore us to our humanity. Our sufferings began a long time ago, and those we would wish them on are too far away. Ti Louze and Gabriel are within earshot of our voices, within reach of our hands. We are cruel by default. Wicked by obligation.

In the face of inextinguishable anger, Gabriel breathes jerkily as he examines his legs carefully. He fears that the lash has left visible traces; he fears his little friends will make fun of him at school. Ti Louze sniffs loudly. She no longer has the words to beg for leniency: 'Please, please...' A trickle of blood runs from the two or three scabs she has caused herself by dabbing at insect bites with an old, worn cloth. Through her tears, Ti Louze calls on death but will have to wait for that wish to be granted. Ti Louze and Gabriel must think that the world is an unfair place, and they're not wrong. Gabriel will get used to it, sooner than he may think. For Ti Louze the game has already been played out, in full. Ti Louze, whose braids are no longer than finger-bones; a true African's head with no future on this island – Ti Louze, so black she is invisible.

A moment later, no doubt weary of this game, Mother asks me to call Paulo, the son of our neighbour Madame Jacques. She doesn't mention Jean-Baptiste or Wiston who live at the other end of the street. While waiting for Paulo, she ceaselessly slaps her lower arms to warm up her blood.

The sky is pink-hued mother-of-pearl, but the night's mood still freezes us to our bones.

Sitting at Mother's feet, I drink my coffee in silence. I think of Fignolé. Where could he possibly have spent the night? Why did he hide that gun behind the cupboard? Why? I think of Luckson. Of the jeans I'll put on this morning. I study my toe nails, my fingernails. My nail varnish, salmon-coloured, is beginning to flake off.

FIVE

I begin my shift at seven o'clock as usual. On arrival, I carry out the same routine tasks, to distance myself from the pain that I always see in the sick who line both sides of the large communal ward as I walk down it.

Gabriel had trouble waking this morning and going over his lessons for school. No doubt there were other images playing out behind his eyelids. There was nothing to be done about it; my fear that night must have crept in between the folds and furrows of his sleep. However, when he woke I was ruthless with the whip. God knows why! A malicious spirit took pleasure in whispering like burning coals: 'The whip never did any harm to a little Negro boy or girl. The whip never did any harm...' And I hit him. And I hit her... 'Fignolé can say whatever grand words he likes about suffering and injustice, but Ti Louze should consider herself lucky that we've taken her away from her peasant life.' And I hit, and I hit. 'A life where she would be dead by now from eating roots and drinking the stagnant water of the ponds.' I hit them until my arm ached, until I was exhausted.

Now I regret using the whip. I regret that I can't undo what I did. This violence was all I had to distance myself as far as I could from my fear. This violence that leaves me with the taste of mud and ash in my mouth. Because of the whip Gabriel appeared not to recognise me – me, his mother – when I made him kiss me as he left the house. It was not until he disappeared at the end of the road that I could resign myself to taking my eyes off him.

Gabriel devours me in silence and he doesn't know it. No-one knows. Gabriel was the beginning of my sleepless nights, my desolate mornings. Gabriel was the beginning of my solitude. A child is the beginning of solitude for all women... But enough of these grand sentiments. This is the turning-point where I, Angélique Méracin, await Joyeuse, my sister Joyeuse, so free, so free...

Walking down the road, I greeted neighbours as I passed: 'Hello, Madame Jacques, Maître Fortuné. Hello Boss Dieuseul, Willio. Hello Wiston, Jean-Baptiste, Altodir, Théolène, all of you.'

Madame Jacques' shop stocks everything we could want in this every-man-for-himself neighbourhood: sugar, which she pours into little paper bags, needles and thread, Palma Christi oil and honey that leave the shelves sticky, antibiotics, products for straightening the hair, lightening the skin, school notebooks and rice, supplied by food for the poor but sold to us by Madame Jacques. Just like she makes us pay for the telephone calls we receive or make on the filthy, malodorous receiver on her counter. Madame Jacques keeps notes beneath her voluminous bosom and impassively deals out strong words to recalcitrant customers, surrounded by the sticky flight of the flies.

Jean-Baptiste was wearing a jacket too narrow for his broad shoulders. He has had a job for a while at the Customs office. He is blessed with luck – the men of the Prophet-President, boss of the Démunis party, don't employ but recruit. Jean-Baptiste imposes the same regime on this collection of houses, like a boss. On Théolène, Altodir and Louidon who, sitting on this pavement, watch the passers-by from sunrise to sunset, picking their teeth, scratching their ears, whistling at girls and laughing as they rub their knees. Slapping their thighs. Opening and closing their legs. Boss Dieuseul, taciturn and with a sombre regard, is the only one to spend the brightest part of the day claiming that whatever will happen, he has already seen it. That what has already happened is nothing compared to what awaits us.

Here, every smile has its measure, every word its weight. In this neighbourhood we play out muted wars. Wars without victory, without outcomes and without glory. These are petty wars. Wars in which, every day, we examine our defeats a little more closely. Wars of the vanquished, whose history is nothing but a great dark play, full of noise, fury and blood. A history that makes us hate our very presence in the world, the black humiliation of our skin.

In the central space between the beds aligned on either side of the ward, I move with a steady pace, chest squared, feet turned slightly outward, to prevent myself from being caught by the exhaustion that I drag behind me like a convict's ball and chain. This stiffness in the way I walk comes also from everything my nostrils breathe in between these walls, these images like a release of wild birds. From all that my ears have heard expressed by mouths twisted by pain. From that which my hands have touched, living or dead. A great tangle of nerves constantly re-awoken beneath my skin. It's amazing that I'm still sane. Surprising that madness has not devoured me to the marrow.

Joyeuse says I must have swallowed a broomstick, the way I walk so straight, without the slightest sway of my behind, without that rowboat roll that is expected of a woman, a real woman, so she says. Especially a woman from round here. She often seasons her own bitterness with a hint of contempt.

'Unbelievable,' she repeated again this morning, as she applied her lipstick and twirled in front of her mirror.

SIX

I'm hardly able to drag my thoughts away from the metallic object on top of the cupboard. I hardly dare put a name to it in my head. Too many questions torment me and threaten to become an obsession. Why this gun? Does Fignolé believe he's in danger right now? Why hasn't he spoken of it? Why did he leave it in that cupboard if he's in fear of his life? Perhaps he's not himself a target but he's protecting a friend? Who knows? I open my bag quickly, thinking to find an answer to my questions in those few bits of paper left by Fignolé. There is a telephone number, Ismona, the forename of his girlfriend, written in capitals, the district of Martissant underlined in red and a line of verse: *The heart yearns for a bullet while the throat raves of a razor.* Beneath, in small, fine writing, Mayakovsky. Knowing Fignolé as I do, none of it is written at random. Everything has a reason, which I will come to decipher. Fignolé learned all these grand, fine words on a few forays into gatherings in Pacot, Laboule or Pétion-Ville where, seated on comfortable sofas, they enacted the Revolution surrounded by glasses of wine and the sounds of the trumpet of Miles Davies or Wynton Marsalis.

Fignolé, why make us breathe at such giddy heights? Recalcitrant, rebellious Fignolé, inhabited by poetry, crazy about music. Fignolé has no place on this island where disaster has broken spirits. Fignolé, can you hear me? Pass through the lightning and the fire of this city unharmed if you will, but come back to us… Come back to us soon. Unhurt, uninjured. More alive than a living soul in this land ever was. Fignolé, can you hear me?

I leave the house at the same time as Mother, who refused to wear the dress with little sun-yellow flowers that I bought for her during the last sales at Madame Herbruch's shop. Not content with merely refusing to wear this dress, Mother tied a scarf round her head like a peasant. I didn't dare say anything to her. She had that expression I know so well, that 'you don't want to cross me' expression. No loa had yet ridden her, but even so, she had already escaped me, her mouth firmly shut like a tomb. Her eyes turned towards the Invisibles.

This evening I'll do her hair and that's all. My fingers moist with Palma Christi oil, I'll take pleasure in undoing her little plaits one by one and then putting her hair up in a single braid above her nape. She'll protest at first, but she'll let me do it. As always. This is an established ritual between us, which ultimately pleases us both. It always has, since childhood when, as night fell, she would invoke Grandfather Saintilhomme, whose legends bind us all to one another. Grandfather, whom the god Agoué came to find one day to take him to Guinea underwater. Or the tales in which the fish are clothed in phosphorescent seaweed. Where ogres devour children. Where stars can be caught in the palm of your hand. She would tell these stories until the day the blood ran between my thighs for the first time. Looking me right in the eye, Mother asked me to be on guard with boys from that moment on, and stopped talking to me. I mean, really talking to me. It was a parenthesis of silence. The truce of adolescence. The end of those hours, warm and so full of sweetness. She was content to reassure herself that each new moon brought me my share of moist, warm blood.

One day she inserted an authoritative finger to reassure herself that my body had not yet been breached, was no wound open to the breeze. She never did it again. I understood quickly that there was a connection between this blood, the shadowy triangle of my thighs, and the men who made Mother appear more beautiful sometimes, a dancing flame in everyone's eye, her hips as if released, when I would get home from school and our bed would exude a scent of amber and kelp.

I also experienced the discomfort, the unease of having a place in that school among girls who were strangers to me. Mother was jubilant at the idea of her daughter's unexpected advance towards that world of stucco, lace and frills, but never imagined the violence it would imply for her, never. Right from the start, I had refused to assume the role of an innocent who would steal cheap jewellery and only realise too late. I had chosen to be a thief of stones of deceptive brilliance. One who knows it and continues to do it, with no regrets, without useless nostalgia. In my adolescence I had a volcano inside me, which I ignited myself, without saying a word, every morning. Now this volcano will never be extinguished, Mother and I have merely changed places and roles.

I'm twenty-three years old and I'm the strongest.

Mother lets me do her hair and listens, sitting between my knees or with me standing behind her. We have re-emerged from our silence. I talk to her of my twenties which are like an itch, of my great hunger for life, of my certainty that there is no-one to complain to about the battering and hurt the world will bring.

Mother knows like no other how to keep to herself in her silence. She knows how to love us in her silence like the warmth of the earth. Like the light which enwraps the world. Hers is a love against which all the fury, all the noise of others are as nothing. I know it as I know that no-one will love Ti Louze. No-one. As I know that hard, cold cruelty also lives in the hearts of the defeated – a certainty that Fignolé always opposed with a hundred explanations and a thousand boastful answers.

Madame Jacques stops us on the threshold of her shop. She wants to reassure us about Fignolé.

'He'll come back later,' she says sharply. 'Paulo is sure of it.'

This morning, Madame Jacques does not look good. The cares of the last few weeks have given her a sunken, tattered appearance. This morning, Madame Jacques is older than all the women who walk barefoot in the dust of the Old Testament. Older than Rebecca. Older than Judith. Older than Jezebel or Sara. Further on, Maître Fortuné rushes up in front of Mother, contenting himself with taking her clammy hands into his and inclining his head towards her breast. Apart from Madame Jacques and Maître Fortuné, mother does not confide in the other neighbours. Certainly not in Madame Descat, our neighbour on the right, recently moved in to the neighbourhood. A woman with an opulent bosom, she has visibly lightened the skin of her face with lashings of abrasive creams. Madame Descat is one whom we don't know well enough to take into our confidence but know too well to share our misfortunes with. Madame Descat receives visitors who are no doubt enthralled by the falseness of this grimelle who has arrived and who looks down on us with an air of authority. Mother gives Madame Descat broad smiles, which are returned with the same hypocrisy. Not me. She can see from my expression that I'm not afraid to get in with my teeth first before I can be bitten.

The present-day mistrust creeps through their veins like a seeping liquid, thicker than that of the mistrust there has always been – the mistrust that the older people always obliged us to maintain towards those who resemble us like peas in a pod. Together with misfortune, this mistrust is the only inheritance to which we, the defeated, are truly entitled. It certainly does not count among our losses, but our gains. It's not hard to see why!

Mother endlessly repeats that the neighbours are not what they were. And that we are fortunate to have Maître Fortuné.

'Without someone like Maître Fortuné you couldn't last in this city. There would be no future here.'

Maître Auguste Fortuné is able to set you up with a clandestine source of water or electricity in less time than it would take you to ask for it, or to procure for you a certificate of birth, death or any kind of qualification. Tall and strong like the trunk of a mapou, with stooped shoulders and furtive eyes, he makes his way through hardships at a steady pace. Maître Fortuné is not a master of anything but muddling-through and trickery. Maître Fortuné exists only to satisfy himself that not a single centime will line the pockets of the State. Not a single one. A great usurer, Maître Fortuné lends on the black market. Maître Fortuné is the fruit of a blend of races, all the virtues of which we have rejected, retaining only the faults. He has made his place in our great disorder like a fish in water and revels in having the whole wide ocean to swim in. He has thrown a thick veil over his past, a veil that no-one lifts. Malicious tongues say that he embezzled the funds of a minister and came out of it by a feat of conjuring. Others claim that after making a living by running a brothel in Cap-Haïtien, he stripped a few forsaken widows in Curaçao of their assets and entertained a number of bored housewives in Fort-de-France. So why did he end up among us? We will never know.

A true chameleon, Maître Fortuné knows how to assume the colours of whoever is in power, tinting his tongue and his brain. But it is impossible to talk of his soul. For activities of the kind he undertakes, Maître Fortuné is not burdened with a soul, fortunately!

Fortunately for him, and for us who live in this neighbourhood of houses that are permanent but twisted,
half-finished, half-painted, displaying their metal guts
like shaggy hair. This neighbourhood to which we have
escaped but only just, with the fetid breath of alleyways
which, elsewhere, further downtown, among the
shanties, are sickening. We live in a place like a fruit that
is half worm-eaten, half rotten, where eager teeth may
yet bite. But all the same, we live in a neighbourhood of
the defeated. With plenty of cause for unblemished, rich,
deep happiness and with other things that are ugly, terrible and yet so human.

Now I think on, Paulo has not mentioned Vanel, the
young drummer in the band. I love Vanel, I love his
fragility. Vanel licks a great internal wound, like an
injured dog; a great wound that no-one sees. A few years
ago now, Monsieur Perrin, a teacher at the Toussaint
school, praising his intelligence and his talent to his
mother and his aunt, offered to take him in to his house
on the pretext of shaping a great future for him. Once
under the roof of this benefactor, he was taught neither
grammar nor multiplication tables, even less drawing or
music, but intimacy with someone of the same sex.
Monsieur Perrin swore to him between breaths, shorts
around his ankles, penis extended in his fingers, that this
would be better than with girls. Ever since, Vanel has
vacillated between the two sexes. And he hides his game
from everyone – especially the boys of the football team
who meet at Théolène's. He knows full well they'd give
him a hard time if they learned that men sometimes ask
him to play the man and often the woman. Only my
friend Lolo and I know. When Vanel is not making my
head spin with confidences or giving me an account of
the latest episode of our favourite TV soap beneath the
cramped gallery in front of the house, we are laughing
like two accomplices who don't believe in Hell, who

believe that the earth is a brutal paradise. I love Vanel, I love his fragility, his long lashes which make his eyes look moist.

I put one foot in front of the other. But my questions chase their tails like a trese ruban dance and come to worry at my secrets, rake out my grey stone. Fignolé, where are you? God, I want to know where you're hiding!

SEVEN

Joyeuse's words do not reach me. She is deceiving herself and doesn't know it. I often smile inside at the complacent pride of her ignorance. Joyeuse with her bird's brain can't imagine the experiences I've accumulated. No, she can't. The experiences that the years have woven into the redness of my flesh and the darkness of my bones. I always make sure that the face I show people is that of an unharmed creature, one who has come through life like passing through the holes in a colander, leaving all the hardships behind. Even the keenest eye would have to look twice, several times before beginning to understand. I mean to really understand. To understand that beneath the apparent ingenuousness of my skin lurk the moving scales of a strange beast, that I'm a woman whose days are made up of a feverish waiting – feverish to the point of pain. A woman exhausted by desire for unknown men. A sinner! But I'm rambling, I'm rambling... What evil thoughts, Angélique! What evil thoughts! I don't really know myself any more. Perhaps without the help of God and Pastor Jeantilus I would simply return to what I always was.

I know things I will not say. I also have my suspicions. Suspicions, observations, guesses, conclusions. My soul on edge, mouth closed tight, ears pricked like a listening trumpet. I don't tell anything to anyone. With a naked madness, yet I have never been closer to lucidity. Cold and sharp like a knife. Sometimes I aim at my target totally unnoticed and allow myself a sharpened arrow, the type that arouses Mother's curiosity. Which leaves Fignolé apparently indifferent, but which makes my sister Joyeuse howl. Only the day before yesterday she was in such a fury that she shouted at me that I was nothing but a sanctimonious woman prematurely aged where I stood, like a stunted tree. I put on my most innocent expression while gloating inside as I always do. There was nothing else for it; spitefulness soothes me. Powerless to drive out the true words buried in my night, incapable of making the exact gestures that would restore my life with a flick of the wrist, I'm caught up in a mechanism of hatred. And so I allow myself the spite which opens up my prisons, breaks away my chains.

This is the same mechanism that drove Fignolé, as a frenzied crowd gathered to herald the return of the leader of the Démunis, to plunder a wealthy-looking house uptown with a gang of friends from our neighbourhood, Paulo, Jean-Baptiste and Wiston. Their sincere belief was that they could escape for ever the hopeless pain of a country that was lost, debased, trampled underfoot. They finished up with a new injection of hope that was quickly forgotten. Visibly ecstatic, they rejoined the gang of wild down-and-outs. A noisy, foul-smelling, disobedient crowd. A crowd white-hot with alcohol and weed and goodness knows what else. Fires rose up from barricades thrown up in haste. In a fever. In the vibrant breath of the lambis, the conch horns. The drums filled the city with the warrior rhythms of ancient Africa. A powerful song like a river caused the crowd to sway, arms moving, hair in disarray, legs spread like people possessed. Men, women, children, old folk: all were going wild from that blend of anger with joy and hunger. Those who were running barefoot were indifferent to the pain caused by the smashed bottles, twisted pieces of metal and fragments of wood that littered the ground. In a furious tumult they carried off everything they could lay their hands on – mattresses, household appliances, works of art, like trophies from a great battle. It was said that one man's body lay prone in the entrance to his house. Truth or rumour? Who knows? Executed, lynched. Or perhaps both. He was dead there, on the pavement, guilty beneath a harsh, stiff sun like fate. Intoxicated by that frenzied crowd, did Fignolé, too, throw a rock or step over the body without even noticing? I never knew that, either.

When he returned home at the end of the afternoon, a television set carried on his head, I laid into him. A flood of reprimands gushed from my breast. My anger had such a minimal effect on him that it ended up working itself out. And as my anger calmed, I looked at Fignolé with an admiration that surprised even me. Deep inside, a strange fire suddenly ignited and began to crackle. And I felt that it was crackling because I approved of him. Yes, I approved of him. I understood on that day that there is no wrong in turning malicious when you are enslaved. When there is no point to your life, nor to the lives of all those like you since the beginning of the world, and one day a moment will come when a man will show you the way out. And that way will be so narrow, so low, so dark, that it will swallow you whole, your head down. And I lowered my head. And perhaps I would do it again. Who knows?

The shame in the Bible, that of Pastor Jeantilus' sermons, only came that evening to add itself to my hatred – slowly, but without ever succeeding in reducing it to silence. Ever. It was that hatred which, during the following days, fed my delight in knowing that the people beyond my reach had lost something. At least once, and at the hands of one of my own. I remember singing very loudly in church the following Sunday, eyes closed, my body reeling from side to side, arms waving above my head. In order to smother the spite with words and music and not to give it another chance. But it was in vain. Remorse had never been able to make its nest in the depths of my being, the place where no-one but me goes. The place from where a glimmer of light sometimes comes to dance, lighting up my eyes when I look at myself in the mirror and when I light a fire in my life. For a few seconds. Just a few magnificent seconds.

We still have no news of Fignolé. No phone call. No message. Nothing. Absolutely nothing. Joyeuse has maintained that little self-satisfied expression and that false serenity that winds me up so much. Yet even though she has not been taken into her brother's confidence, she must surely have her suspicions, must have noticed some clues. I slipped Mother a gourde note. She will use it to pay Madame Jacques for the phone call I will make to her from the hospital cafeteria. I've promised and I want to know...

EIGHT

Standing on the front step of the house, as ever I have had to call Lolo several times before she finally came over to join us, Mother and me. Lolo is never on time, but Lolo is Lolo. She's my accomplice, my sister in the frenzy of living. Lolo is a vixen. No other girl in this fight-with-your-claws-out-to-stay-alive neighbourhood knows as well as Lolo how to benefit from every kind of situation. No-one knows as well as she does how to drive a bargain with such self-assurance and cunning on the pavements of this city as she does – a T-shirt, a pair of shoes, jeans, sandals. No-one can string together as quickly as she does a barrage of bad language forceful enough to strip you of your trousers or pants, enough even to shock a brothel-keeper. No-one can. I love Lolo because she is totally on the sunny side, her outlook totally on pleasure. And when I'm having a bad day, and tend too much towards the direction of the moon, she draws me towards her fire.

'Too many books,' she likes to say to me, 'too much thinking going on in that little head of yours, sister.'

When we were teenagers, our closeness was sealed by French songs, the lyrics of which we would write down in the pages of school exercise books. Lying on our stomachs, flat out on the ground or with our knees bent, legs swinging gently backwards and forwards, we would hum all those lyrics imbued with a blue-tinged happiness. We dreamt of a rich, handsome man, preferably white, who would come to take us away from this seedy neighbourhood in a luxury car, or why not a plane or a yacht?

> *If you didn't exist*
> *I think I would invent you*

Finding these songs too unrealistic, we swapped them for the reggae of Bob Marley and Janesta, the merengue of Djakout Mizik and the drums of Boukman Eksperyans and Azor. In the recent past, mothers, sisters and wives had found us charming, but that was no longer the case – not at all. Lolo and I are now a formidable team in the face of public condemnation. A tough duo. Adversity is the fire that heats us and welds us together. We're like two Sioux or Cheyennes who have sealed a pact, a bond forged from the blood of our wrists. Virtuous souls, sensitive souls, steer clear! We are two killers let loose on the streets of Babylon. Two wildcats lying in wait in this voracious city.

Since we have been of an age to attract the attention of men, the women of the neighbourhood have taken to pressing their lips together tightly as we pass, imagining excruciating tortures that would leave us hideous and twisted. But in vain – here we are, full of life, and determined to stay that way for a long time to come. Given over to their resentment and whispered allegations, they forbid their children, sons and daughters alike, from talking to us for too long. What stratagems would they not employ to steer their teenagers with their turbulent hormones towards nocturnal dreams that don't feature us? Instead of benefiting from our blazing otherness, young women of our age, Angélique included, prefer to add their sad voices to the cries of the pack. See them waiting for a man they will never have, going to church in the hope that one day God will grant their prayers. Lolo and I have not set foot in a church for years.

However, we have known, but never once held on to, some of those men whom these women await in vain on bended knee with their eyes turned to heaven. Like Angélique, they still have not understood that God does not get involved in things, if He knows how to give at all. So we help Him, that's all.

With these thoughts in my head I walk on, one step at a time, Mother on one side of me, Lolo on the other. A yellow T-shirt shows off the shape of Lolo's breasts to good effect and a pair of jeans moulds her buttocks. Only a black woman could have such breasts, such buttocks, and yet be as slender as a reed. At the end of the road, the males of the neighbourhood, all ages together, watch us pass, licking their chops. It's a matter of being aware, senses on edge, waiting for the clacking of the pieces in a great domino game. Hours later, the noise of these dominos will be drowned out by stormy discussions at a football match, the appearance of supernatural creatures, men with goats' horns, a smiling bullock with a gold tooth, or by suggestive laughter about their masculine prowess. It is hard to hear these voices and this laughter without thinking of the pain which hides behind the eyes, beneath the chest, in the small of the back and along calves weary from running towards nothing. These voices and this laughter also explain why misfortune always finds as much space as it needs on this island to spread its wings and grow, but not enough space to be alone. And so we rock back and forth like the movement of a rocking chair. It's crazy, the things we wait for in this country! When there is nothing to be done about it. Crazy! And time goes by. And time goes by... And the earth gradually, slowly decomposes ... But I, Joyeuse Méracin, I don't wait. I do and I undo.

Wiston and the others have set up a table and four rickety chairs right beneath the sign announcing Le Bon Berger, Boss Dieuseul's forge. From time to time one or other of them will leave the gaming table to go off and hang out beneath other roofs or sow their wild oats, then return an hour or so later. Or the next day. In three days. Or perhaps never. In any case, all the men on this island are just passing through. Those who stay longer are just a little more permanent, that's all. On this island there are only mothers and sons.

His back against a wall, right leg folded up beneath him, Jean-Baptiste draws slowly on his cigarette. Jean-Baptiste is seen to keep an eye on them. He reigns over this small kingdom. Jean-Baptiste is a petty king who likes the smell of the herd. His flock may be idle to the point of inertia, but the arrangement is that Boss Dieuseul works solely for him as blacksmith, painter, electrician and divine healer. Hammer in hand, Boss Dieuseul raises his emaciated face with its drawn-out chin. It is the moment when he will predict – a prediction that is met with indifference – that men will writhe in torment, women will wallow in the stench of their own suffering, rivers will be swollen with entrails and blood, and whatever else… Then his protruding eyes, which seem to bulge from his face as a result of some distant suffering, are once more fixed on his hands.

Jean-Baptiste turns his whole upper body. Passing before him on the arms of Mother and Lolo, I meet two eyes drunk with the force of looking at me. Jean-Baptiste can't resist looking at me, he just can't. Jean-Baptiste doesn't look at me, he undresses me. Deep inside himself, Jean-Baptiste thinks I don't choose. That I will lie down beneath the first man who comes along and snaps his fingers. He expects that all he has to do is click with his thumb and middle finger to have me fall at his feet. Mother's eyes linger on him as if to say, 'You will have to dance on my grave before you can have this girl who walks by my side, young man.'

Jean-Baptiste does not dare look Mother in the eye

and turns his head away. I suspect that Jean-Baptiste, gasping and panting like an old dog, has served up to Ti Louze that threat he keeps concealed in his pants, after cornering her one afternoon between two doorways. Jean-Baptiste is a pig.

I leave Mother and Lolo, intrigued, at the end of the road and slip away for a few seconds, hoping that the neighbourhood's only phone box is working. I dial the number written on Fignolé's scrap of paper and reach a voicemail service asking me to leave a message. Naturally, I don't. Best to be careful. I leave any further attempt till later. Lolo and I accompany Mother to the tap-tap station. She takes her leave of us, but only listens with half an ear to our recommendations. 'If you hear any shots, if... if...' She nods and that is all. We go our different ways, Lolo and I uptown, Mother towards the crowded suburb where Aunt Sylvanie lives.

Aunt Sylvanie's neighbourhood is on the edge of an even poorer area – on this island, poverty has no limits. The deeper you dig, the more you will find poverty even greater than your own. And so, between Sylvanie and that which doesn't yet have a name there is merely a small area of trapped water, full of silt and mud, enough to turn your stomach. Over there, on the other side, is the place where lives are held in balance between the peelings of everything that can be eaten, animal carcases, the incontinence of the old folk, children's faces grimed with snot and that bitter water rejected even by starving stomachs. Alongside the dogs and the pigs, sinister shadows often emerge. Backs bent, they blend in with the animals. When they are not fighting them for the scraps, they are furtively rooting in the stinking, rotten rubbish on either side. I would often find myself leaning forward, eyelids half-closed, hand on my forehead to get a better view and convince myself that those creatures were not dogs, nor pigs, but human beings like you or me; men, women, children, old people who have no choice but to get up in the morning, live, eat, make babies and see to their needs. Hundreds and thousands of souls come to the city as if to paradise, only to find nothing but this hell under an open sky. Ti Louze can consider herself lucky to have found us. If God created this world, I hope he is tortured by remorse.

From the other bank I often look across at this world like someone who, in the midst of battle, just escaped by means of a well-sharpened machete blade or a hail of bullets from a submachine gun, and is now unable to believe their luck. Anyone who once sets foot in that district will from that moment know why the streets sometimes spread their legs for the highest bidder or shed blood with the calendars. It's impossible not to know, impossible!

The night was punctured by the crackling of gunfire. The city, pregnant with a hideous beast, fought an insidious war. On the orders of the boss of the Démunis, armed bands in the outlying districts blended in with the forces of order, once more to take hold of the city and liquidate the insurgents one after the other. They are tracked down street by street, alley by alley. The more fortunate ones might come away riddled with bullets. They behead the less fortunate ones, showing off the heads at arm's length or on the end of a pole, burning them like torches or mutilating them and feeding them to the pigs.

Why did Fignolé underline Martissant in red? Why is Ismona's name written in capital letters? And that telephone number? And why these lines of verse? What is the connection between them? The connection with the rest of it? A long day awaits…

NINE

Icontinue my shift as if nothing has happened. I administer drops, distribute tablets, instruct the auxiliaries to change dressings. One of them, taken on just a week ago, can hardly tell left from right, so I have to oversee everything. Taking blood samples, wielding thermometer and syringes. This morning I am unlikely to be vigilant enough. I'm too worried about Fignolé. I'm concerned for Mother.

Despite our warnings, she wanted to consult Aunt Sylvanie. 'No-one and nothing can stop me.'

As recently as last week she sat herself on the back of a moto-taxi and sped off, heading alone across that part of the city where thousands of bodies mill about in a mix of bustle and lethargy between the pavements and the road, defying the tap-taps and bus traffic forging ahead at full speed in an earsplitting racket. You would run away without hesitation if you didn't fear the crowded pavements with their risk of entangling your feet in other calloused feet, the feet of beggars, carters and idlers, all battling for space. And so you dodge with agility between three Francis mangos, four large bunches of bananas and two pots of peas spread out for sale on the ground. A cocktail of smells pervades the air and threatens to suffocate you. The scent of tobacco. Rancid oil. The peelings of fruit and vegetables. Offcuts of meat fought over by battered dogs. Sweat from armpits and between thighs. Mother crosses this flood, knocking against legless cripples, children with flies teeming around their nostrils, women as thin as nails, bumping into the lame and the blind, finally reaching the stall at the far end, the one where machetes, rigoises and knives are hung on display, before heading for Sylvanie's neighbourhood.

Mother has an unshakeable belief that the Spirits who dwell in flasks, bottles and gourds wait at Aunt Sylvanie's house to cure ills. To prophecy. To explain mysteries. That Aunt Sylvanie knows how to awaken them to apply a soothing balm to all those who visit her.

This morning, having drunk her cachiman infusion, Mother summoned Paulo to her. He went out with Fignolé yesterday evening to who knows where, his guitar under his arm. But listening to Paulo's words we were none the wiser. He looked like someone who had not got a wink of sleep all night. Someone afraid. And above all, someone who had smoked a whole field of marijuana all to himself. His Rasta dreadlocks covered half of his face. All the while he was talking to us, he never stopped looking towards the door and raising himself on his toes when not bluntly turning away. You would think he was being watched. When he was not turning in all directions he kept his head down. Paulo knows something but does not want to speak. No-one could convince me otherwise. He gabbled three or four confused sentences about a guitar with strings gone slack, one of the two vocalists being ill and some such. Mother didn't believe a single word of an outpouring he seemed to be inventing on the spot to reassure us. Joyeuse, hands on hips, rebuffed him like only she knows how.

'My dear Paulo, you seem to think I was born yesterday. You've always been one for telling stories. You're not going to make me swallow any old lies.'

The only definite information we were able to drag out of him was that Fignolé left them around ten o'clock, together with Vanel, the group's drummer, and Ismona, heading for Martissant. And then nothing more was heard...

In the hospital corridors distress has left its marks. Electricity cuts have caused the smell of corpses to rise from the morgue and spread this far. For the first time ever, nausea hits me head on. I make an effort to hear human voices, to understand them.

The last time he stayed in this hospital, Fignolé was being eaten away inside by a kind of fever, which froze him and burned him up, all at the same time. Fignolé was trembling, shivering. We had every reason to be eaten by worry. We feared the worst. At mid-day, in the heat of July, with the thermometer recording thirty-five degrees in the shade, I heard his teeth chattering. I immediately changed his sweat-soaked sheets – sheets I'd brought myself to a hospital that has nothing – and dried his shoulders, his chest and his back to stop him getting a chill. A doctor arrived a few days later, an American with a sing-song accent like in the westerns. This was a real stroke of luck for someone like Fignolé, who liked to live his life on the throw of a dice, to thumb his nose at death. The doctor changed his medication and asked if his case could be passed to colleagues in a health centre downtown. But all this I guessed after-wards. The stranger didn't want to talk to him in my presence, under the pretext of the patient's right to dis-cretion.

The fact that Fignolé was an adult.

That all sickness is private.

He waited for acquiescence from me. I looked him straight in the eyes and then turned on my heel and left in silence. Even strangers take me for something I'm not.

It was the same with John and Father André. John, a young American journalist, had followed Fignolé over all the blazing barricades he had raised in order to shout out his hatred of the men in uniform and demand the return of the leader of the Démunis whom they had driven from power. He and Fignolé became inseparable for several long months. Very quickly, Paulo, Wiston and Jean-Baptiste joined them in their dreams of insurrection, their revolutionary projects and their secret meetings of desperados. As for Father André, he gave them his blessing between two Our Fathers and three acts of contrition.

We have known Father André since he arrived from faraway Belgium a few years ago. After looking after the church of St Anne's, he was sent to Solino, the crowded neighbourhood where Aunt Sylvanie lives. He believed I was saintly simply because I had cared for two patients he referred to me, free of charge in their homes. As for John, that was a longer story. Much longer. John got out of a hire car with Fignolé one afternoon. Six foot three, he looked down on us and wished us a good evening with a very gentle smile. This tall blond man, with the thin lips of people from colder climates and inordinately long arms and legs, found it difficult to sit comfortably in the cramped gallery at the entrance to our house. When he arrived, he planted himself in front of Mother who looked at him with an extraordinary intensity. Her astonishment was enough to make Fignolé, Joyeuse and I laugh till our sides split. She admitted later that she had seen in John a striking resemblance to the image of Jesus holding his bleeding heart, which hung on the wall of the living room.

That afternoon, sitting on the step by the entrance to the house, Fignolé could not resist declaring in the tone of someone who had just won first prize:

'John is a friend, an American journalist.'

John put his backpack down beside his chair and began by saying:

'I love this country; I love the poor.'

He made his pronouncement in the way that others

would say I'm a doctor, a plumber or a lawyer.

Before meeting John I had not known it was possible to earn a living by loving the poor, that loving the poor was a profession.

TEN

Fignolé's notes spin round crazily inside me like a carousel. How can I decipher the mystery of that telephone number? And that verse – I'd like to get to the bottom of the significance of that to Fignolé. Though in fact the significance is too evident not to petrify me. The capitals in which he has written Ismona's name reveal the passion that has been taking shape. I felt that, in Ismona, he had found a gentleness and closeness the left him unable to believe his luck – he who, pursued by anxiety, looks for pain to revel in as others would a marvel. To the point of fever, to the point of dizziness. But there he is calling on the bullet and the razor, even if it is despite himself. What was he looking for in the brothels of the Grande-Rue where, behind the bead curtains, on unsavoury mattresses, the sexes come together, mouth to mouth, body to body? The dope and the music haven't cured him of the world. Ismona, his muse under the sun, his sister in the night, can she save him? This morning, I don't believe she can. I don't believe it. Any reassurance will leave Fignolé helpless. He wears despair like a second skin.

I've been worried about Fignolé for too long, not because he smokes joints, not at all, but because of what these joints could lead him to do. I worry myself sick because of his music. Because of his rebelliousness. Because of everything that gets all mixed up and makes too much sense. The music won't tear down the walls, Fignolé. It can't. I'm worried about your height, your weight, your bowel movements, your sex, your perspiration, your tears, your hunger and your thirst. I will put a finger on the place where your heart is wounded and I will stop it from bleeding one second longer! Believe me and come home.

I still can't help connecting all this information to the fact that Fignolé and Paulo met up with the rebels while John, Wiston and Jean-Baptiste didn't. For Wiston and Jean-Baptiste the choice is clearer. It is a choice based on deprivation, a low doorway that obliges the defeated to bow their heads. As for John, he is nothing but a pitiable man who is afraid to leave his illusions behind and who holds onto them by putting up with any kind of horror. The dream has already died where he comes from, on the streets of Seattle or New York, on the receiving end of a baton and a few clouds of tear gas, so he wants to revive it here, whatever the cost. Even at the cost of renouncing himself, even at the cost of sacrificing our lives. He twists and retwists events to make his reports look good and to populate that sham paradise he has invented for himself in his head. In any case, John is risking nothing here, John is losing nothing. He's not at home.

'I'll talk to you about hunger one day, John, about the kind of deprivation that bends backs, that opens thighs, about the arrogance of conquerors and the humiliation of the defeated. I'll tell you what goes on inside the head, the stomach and the genitals of a man who is hungry. What goes on inside the head, the stomach and the genitals of a woman who has nothing to give her children to eat. I'll tell you... One day. I'm the only one here who knows you. Who really knows you, I mean.'

The anxiety gives me an empty feeling and I no longer know what to think or who to think about. About Fignolé who hasn't come home. About Mother, about Angélique or about my youth, which is asking, begging me to let the sun intoxicate me, to roll my hips and wait impatiently for Luckson to drive me wild.

It's been so long since I looked up at the sky. Since I took notice of days drenched with light, flowing towards a languid twilight of mauve and orange. Since I gave myself up to this obstinate, avid city, because of its over-flowing energy, because of its strength that can eat me, swallow me whole. Because of the uniformed school-children who set it ablaze at mid-day. Because of its excesses of flesh and images. Because of the mountains which seem to come forward to engulf it. Because there is always too much. Because of the way it has of taking me and not letting me go. Because of its incendiary men and women. Because... Because...

It has been so long since I laughed until my sides ached, like on those Friday afternoons when I would join the young women of the neighbourhood from whom Lolo and I have now taken over. Between hairdos they would sip fruit juice or pop, running their hands over the thin layer of sweat just above their top lips, or over the occasional droplets forming on the bridges of their noses or foreheads. These girls with their legs like palm trees, their expressive behinds who, when the stickiness became unbearable, sucked or noisily bit into ice cubes by the entrance of the only hairdresser's in the neigh-bourhood. It was an excuse to watch the men go by in rare luxury cars or jealously watch those whom good fortune had placed in these dream machines. I particu-larly liked the evenings when Juanita, the owner of the salon, would prepare for her outings. She would quickly run a comb through her hair, her blow-dry completed in the early afternoon, coating her body with a perfumed veil of Opium, her favourite scent. Then, once she had coloured her eyebrows dark brown to match that mark just beneath her throat, she would adjust her breasts in her push-up bra, slip on a dress, always a very clingy

one, and put on her high-heeled sandals. The moment
would then have arrived when she tuned the radio to her
chosen station and performed a few rumba, cha-cha-cha
or salsa moves to satisfy herself that everything was stay-
ing in place. She would always bring this ritual to an end
shaking with a storm of crazy laughter as if she were
being tickled.

I wait three-quarters of an hour before I am finally
able to jump into a tap-tap. I woke early so as not to be
late and to be in a position to throw myself, claws out,
into the merciless stampede of everyday life. When an
old woman with rough skin, bent back and vacant gums
raises her face to mine as she stands by my side, to tell
me in a conspiratorial whisper: 'Mademoiselle, these are
difficult times. You know, in my day...' I remain
unmoved. Not like me, I know, but I am unmoved.
Because that face and that voice could trap me.
Compassion is a luxury I can't afford. And so I con-
sciously raise a wall between the old woman and myself,
topped with barbed wire, broken glass and a 'Beware of
the Dog' sign in large red letters. As I turn towards her,
I do not notice soon enough the brand new four-by-four
that slows down right in front of Lolo and me.

Dark glasses on his nose, a heavy chain around his
neck, a bracelet on his wrist, rings on his fingers, the
driver, grinning like a rampant dog, offers Lolo and me
a place in his car. He reeks of illicit dealings a mile off. I
do not paint on my coarse smile, straighten my shoulders or push up my chest. I do not accept the offer,
despite the imploring expression of Lolo who always
swoons at the sight of a luxury car. I could have done,
like I would have in those days of lassitude, when, to
make my body sing and lighten the wallet of one of those
arrogant males who rush their pleasure and take urgent
possession like soldiers on a campaign, I would play the
game and win. Slipping away unnoticed ... But last night

Fignolé did not come home. I've been tormented for several weeks by a man. None of my strongly-held beliefs about the species applies to Luckson, not one. I am serious despite myself. Despite my twenty years. Despite my great hunger and love of life, the way you do love it at twenty years of age, with the wings of a bird, a sun-drenched look, a heart ready to travel…

The driver with the detestable smile roars away, making a point of splashing water up in a foul-smelling spray from a puddle right by the pavement. Lolo, who's never at a loss for words, follows him with a barrage of vitriol, insulting every attribute his mother has ever had. Her anger pours out in a torrent of choice words. A few passers-by are already applauding and guffawing. I look at the stained hem of my trousers, Lolo's shoes smudged with mud, and like a distant drone hear the voice of the old woman: 'You see what I was saying, you see…'

More than anything I want her to shut up and leave me alone with my rage. When the tap-tap arrives I elbow my way on with a violence I didn't know I had in me. A huge wave of anger and exhaustion breaks over me. A huge, deep wave that rolls me over, drawing back to leave only foam, beating against me with its great liquid body to make me taste the salt and the sand of powerlessness. It all mixes together and weighs ever heavier. Everything I've lost, people, things, my childhood. Everything I've wished for, that I've never had and never will have. Everything I've wanted to know, that I've never known and never will. I measure the immensity of the void until I no longer remember where I am, where I am going, nor where I have come from. I sit down on the bench behind the driver, the very spot I have set my sights on. I don't feel a thing as the tap-tap sets off and I see, through the window, the little old woman, left standing desperate and lost on the pavement, who will have to wait at least another half-hour beneath a sun that is already baring its teeth. A sun like a curse.

This city has taught me one lesson, only one: never to give up on yourself. Never to let a single sentiment soften your spirit. In place of my heart a lump of hard, crude matter has settled inside my chest, right between my breasts. I recognise my little grey stone. And I breathe heavily as I know with certainty that it will remain firmly fixed in place. On this island, in this city, you have to be a stone. I am a stone.

Wedged into this *tap-tap* I allow myself to be gradually invaded by Lolo's chatter as she sits beside me. All the time showing off her fingers with cherry-red fingernails, she has been boasting to me for a full five minutes, and for the nth time, of the talents of a manicurist who has recently been taken on in the beauty salon where she works and who has unrivalled skills in the application of Chinese acrylic nails. And, placing her fingers right in front of my eyes as the incontrovertible evidence, she adds, 'You should allow yourself this little luxury. Go on, I'll get you credit, you won't regret it.'

My laconic reply clearly doesn't please her. She shrugs, a little vexed.

Lolo has the latest mobile phone clamped to her ear. I'm dying to borrow it from her to dial this mysterious telephone number. But I change my mind. You never know. Lolo talks a lot. Too much. In any case, even now she is already giggling with her new lover, 'her old man' as she calls him. Sixty if he's a day and afraid – afraid of growing old. A man who wants to prove his virility in her velvety youth, in the elixir of her twenty years.

'Well, he pays for everything,' Lolo has told me on numerous occasions, giving me a list of all the things she believes she's entitled to: a trip to Miami, a hair extension à la Naomi Campbell ('Honestly, Joyeuse, these hair extensions are never in the colours you need for those great long tresses like the whites have'), cards for her mobile phone and, of course, clothes – if it's clothes you want, here you are. She confided to me that after her first trip to Miami she would come back so as not to arouse suspicion, but on the second she would disappear into the orange groves of Florida.

'You know full well that misery and I just don't get on. I'm not like all those people we're surrounded by who wait for God, Notre-Dame du Perpétuel Secours, Saint Theresa, Agoué, their boss, the government or the revolution to come to their aid. No-one's going to come and save us, Joyeuse, no-one. So the old man won't see Lolo for dust.'

A month ago, out of curiosity, I asked her, 'Your old man, in what way is he old?'

She replied, concentrating hard, as if trying to find the words to describe an expedition to a far-off land, the Antarctic or the North Pole: 'Old like something that's foreign to me, Joyeuse, how can I tell you…? Something I don't know. Old like the snow, cold like the winter.'

Of course, that day we must have talked about Poupette, who took off two years ago with a French aid worker before our dumbfounded, admiring eyes. She returned a few months ago, rolling her r's, talking with a French accent, dressed like a celebrity and took up residence, if you please, in a hotel up there in the swanky district of Pétion-Ville. Lolo, too, never lost hope of landing a similar rare bird to put a ring on her finger.

'The old man is just the first step on my ladder, Joyeuse.'

And Lolo filled my ears with the things we had all heard as whispered secrets from our mothers, who in turn had heard it from their grandmothers, back as far as the ancestors on their pallets in huts and in the holds of ships. That wherever the imploring master hoped to find an anchoring place for his anguish, somewhere to quench his man's thirst, in the calm bellies of the negresses, their turbulent hips and that moist, hot place between their thighs, they would be able to leave the interminable path of the defeated.

John was no exception. I sensed his collapse as man and conqueror in his fascinated hands, his enquiring tongue, his avid mouth, his impatient sex. He could have cried from it. He called me 'My little charcoal-haired sorceress'. For a long time after his attentions ceased to move me, I continued to allow him to touch me, to explore again and again that black cave inside me. I wanted both to learn the lessons of the flesh and to understand this man, his legacy of conquests and my own strength as one of the defeated. A homecoming like this troubled me. Yes, 'troubled' is the right word. I hadn't yet felt with enough certainty my grey stone in the middle of my chest. I wasn't yet clear-headed enough. Not tough enough, either. I'm still not. Still not... And as if she has read my mind, Lolo has no hesitation in dealing me one of those deadly blows she is so good at: 'The love of mathematics has only ever led to a scholarship to go away and study in France or the United States. And what then? You're wasting your time with Luckson, Joyeuse.'

Perhaps she's right? Perhaps I haven't yet totally rejected the complex background of the defeated, whose history is locked up in this black sea that surrounds our island like a tomb?

Lolo's conversation with her old man this morning revolves around lovers' trysts, sugary thank-yous and a new request for money. A bargaining to which I am only half paying attention when a heavy thump against the door, on the driver's side, makes me turn. The thump is followed immediately by the noise of a breaking window pane. A few passengers shout out and protect their faces. I curl up like a snail against the front seat while a strange, deafening rumble comes up from the street. We fear, with good reason, an ambush like the ones that have been taking place for a few weeks now in every corner of the city. The driver stamps on the accelerator and shoots off. Lolo has not let go of her mobile and tells her old man in the minutest detail the misadventure we are in the middle of experiencing. I know her well enough to be sure that she has found here the perfect excuse to raise the stakes later on when she sees him. Later on... That's Lolo all over.

The first emotional moments over, the driver slips in a music cassette. His intention is to prevent any comments by the passengers on the incident we have just experienced, and also to lead us, dancing, to the shores of forgetfulness. The voice of star singer Djakout Mizik ends up getting the better of that fear that for so long has thrown its huge black veil over our city. We lift up the veil, and for a brief time light once again bathes the world. And the things of this world appear to return to their proper place. We allow ourselves to be led by this electrified compas sound which tells us in a rhythmic language not to worry, that money is easy, that life is good and that Djakout Mizik has found the recipe for happiness.

ELEVEN

We gave John the love he wanted. In our own way. Deep down, we were delighted by this man, Fignolé's find. The real spoils of war. And on his second visit Mother took him by the hand and stood him in front of the image of the Sacred Heart of Jesus. Here, she touched him two or three times in succession on his beard and his hair to ensure that he made the connection between this Christ hung on the wall and himself. Mother knows how to do it, I can assure you. She knows how to use her charm to maintain her world. He burst out laughing, revealing his white, neat teeth, and kissed Mother on her cheek. He must have found her charming and exotic.

John arrived ten years ago with a contingent of American soldiers during the second occupation of an island where there has since been no-one but subjects returning with their tails between their legs or losers leaving on their knees. Subjects and losers passing one another in a joint humiliation. What could they do, a race whose bosses, too, had at that point been conquered and humiliated, but themselves become part of that daily, banal disaster? Who on this island would not like to get the better of a foreigner, whether a pastor, aid worker or humanitarian? Previously, there had only been the white Blancs; now we have the black Blancs. The Blancs have brought us unhappiness with one hand and promises of happiness with the other. Who, if they are normal, would not want some of this extravagant thing known as happiness that you see gleaming in the distance? Always in the distance. And it was in order to prove to us that this happiness was within reach that John shared some of our meagre meals, paid for Mother's prescriptions and during a really lean period even agreed to settle up for the funeral of a cousin who didn't actually exist. We pocketed the money in silence. He guessed at the subterfuge but played the game to appease his guilty conscience at being the messenger of the gods. More than anything else on earth he wanted Joyeuse. And the first black Republic got women down on their knees for a few dollars, a meal, some squares of chocolate. John looked at Joyeuse, he looked at her and was barely able to restrain himself from sinking his teeth into this morsel of sweet flesh and devouring her before our eyes. And Joyeuse sensed this. Joyeuse was already so different from me. Full-figured, curvaceous. So sure of herself. So shameless and so sexual. Yes, the word is out. That's what Joyeuse is. Sexual. With all the connotations that go with it, and everything you can guess from it. She fired John up from head to toe like a torch. As young as she was when John came into our lives, her body still uncertain, Joyeuse already knew about the power of that thing she was well aware she carried between her thighs. Every time John visited she would take great care, watched by his mesmerised eyes, to wrap herself up, to build an impenetrable wall of silence or to laugh out loud, all out of breath from running. John was flattered by the agitation he caused in Joyeuse, this young, tantalising Black, this little fairy with a thousand magic spells, with eyes that shone like embers, with her enchanting backside. As for me, I was watching for the moment when John would weaken or bite. I could imagine the film, tinged with coffee, sugar cane and honey, that John was playing in his head, himself a novice among novices, he who, back in his white America, had never gone near anyone like Joyeuse except on a bus or at the checkout of a shop. John had an obstinate, stubborn taste for this forbidden fruit and would salivate at the slightest glimpse of her. And I, Angélique Méracin, I said nothing, as ever.

Joyeuse feigned innocence that afternoon when I arrived home earlier than usual from the hospital and caught them by surprise, alone in the house. Mother had gone to Aunt Sylvanie's and was not due back until the following day. Fignolé must have been yet again at one of those high-school meetings learning how to remake Haiti and the world. Entering through the gate, I noticed John's bag on the porch. I was not wicked enough to open the living-room door even though I had a key. Out of a sense of modesty on their behalf, I went down the narrow passage to the backyard, where I intentionally made a loud noise rattling the large plastic bowl that held the pans and plates. Joyeuse opened the door onto the backyard a few minutes later and with all the boldness I'd always known she had in her, said to me, leaning against the door frame: 'John's here. He's helping me with my English homework.'

'Of course,' I replied, with the same straight face as hers.

But she couldn't care less whether or not I believed her. Joyeuse had already understood that music which spins men around, and had set herself to playing it with talent. Even now I don't know whether it was a matter of caution on John's part or calculation on Joyeuse's that saved us from raising a little mulatto bastard. I just don't know.

During these early visits, bent over his notebook, John had drunk in our every word and religiously taken notes. Our lives were summarised in hastily-scribbled letters, and would seem a world away to people force-fed with words and images. People who would suffer yet another shock and who would be quick to chase us from their hearts because we were no longer bearable – enough, enough!

I didn't particularly like this constant attention to our slightest movement. I got the impression that we were like those urine or blood samples that specialists examine in hospital laboratories for microbes, to confirm or tackle infections. He believed that there was some great complicity between him and me, simply because I cared for the sick and the poor in the only public hospital in the city. In fact I was only there because I hadn't found anything else to do and there were five mouths to feed at home. I only ever dreamt of being elsewhere, that place John had been born into, thousands of kilometres from that shabby hospital on this cursed island. And to make himself love us even more, John imagined us even poorer than we were, and thought of me as someone even more devoted than I was in reality. That was the wonderful film that John and many like him, born beneath benign skies in fine neighbourhoods, play in their heads. Every day, all the time. Mother and I were not fooled, but played along with it, each for our own reasons. But Joyeuse and Fignolé both played a role in John's film, even though they didn't realise it. And at the time it was better like that.

The years passed by. And as always, the euphoria of the first hopes had faded in the face of a world where everyone knew their place in the general hardship. In the eternal postponement of the seasons. With no tomorrows. As for John, he found reasons and scapegoats in all the excesses of the leader of the Démunis, full explanations for all the evils of our island. Today, Fignolé is up against John, up against those at whose side he risked his life for a dream he has left behind since the Démunis party, following the return of its leader, its prophet, has become ten times richer than all the parties of the Rich. Since too much blood has flowed. This blood has dragged Fignolé further into its night. And he sways in anger before that barbarism that wears the face of the Law. An anger from which he will not emerge unharmed. I can feel it.

I carry on with my morning shift. We have fewer resources each day. I'm not really sure what to say to the woman I'm standing in front of, whose back is peeling, the flies buzzing round her in a crazy saraband. She has not been able to move unaided for several weeks now. Several weeks during which the auxiliaries, whose heart is no longer in the job, have been overtaken by events.

TWELVE

Packed into the tap-tap, a veritable disco on wheels, we finally make our way, half deaf, to the city centre. We are deceiving ourselves with this here-and-now, but we are happy with it. We are travelling behind a celebratory front, a carnival of pain, waiting for Port-au-Prince to swallow us up whole once again. The danger is there, lurking in the shadows. We thumb our noses at it. The day mocks us mercilessly, the blue of the sky looks down coquettishly on us. We reflect it all back, and more. We are out to lead life on, to grab from it more than it wants to give. We are out to get the measure of the sun.

My rage has melted away somewhat. But the anxiety is still there, fixing me with a great menacing stare. I don't want this snivelling distress. My tongue, my ears, my eyes, the palms of my hands – all have such a taste for life. I'll find out in the end where Fignolé spent the night. Perhaps he wanted to have Ismona all to himself, to find the taste of sand and stars in a city that has for so long renounced its enchantments, its magic.

As I turn all these questions over and over, I remember that morning when Fignolé asked me for money. I had just been paid and I gave in. The next day he came home with a packet under his arm. The colour of the paper this packet was wrapped in, its shape, the whole thing suddenly comes back to me. The questions take a crazy turn and end up racing away. They threaten to suffocate me. I breathe deeply three times in succession, wedged right into my seat, and I avoid their snares one by one. Anything is better than all these questions, even the wait for Luckson. The wait seems so trivial in the face of calamity, but it is mine. I allow the images, the smells and the light to awake in me another morning, hints of a morning so secret, so unexpected, so overwhelming in the deepest part of me. These images, these smells and this light from elsewhere are those of absence, of deprivation.

Of a man.

A man alone.

An ordinary man.

A man, the hope of my days. The desire of my nights. A man who is eating away my life. A man crouching in the languid space between my hips. A man whose absence descends sweetly down to the tops of my thighs.

A man who hasn't achieved anything special. Who hasn't discovered any unknown land. A man who will not be giving his name to any street, any square. Who is still alive, who breathes somewhere in this city, and who may have forgotten me. Whom I should already have forgotten. This light comes from deep inside his eyes. These smells are those of his hand right next to my face and the blood on that hand.

This light and these smells have not left me since that day when we had all been woken, like today, by volleys of shots and with the same resignation, the same ordinary-day anger beneath our breasts. Lolo, my friend, my accomplice, had joined me a few minutes before. She and I were waiting for the stream of cars and tap-taps to stop at the traffic lights at the bottom of John Brown Avenue, one of the rare sets of lights that were still working. Two youths in uniform, running full pelt, hurled abuse against the Démunis and the party's leader. A shiver ran through the crowd. Lolo and I exchanged looks and immediately feigned indifference. Good sense was paramount. However, I followed the young lads with

my eyes, with blissful admiration, while all around me I
saw that faces were closing up. The crowd speeded up
visibly. Once at the other side of the road, Lolo and I ran
until we were out of breath. Other voices, more and
more of them, louder and louder, joined those of the students. Shots rang out. And a henchman, lying in wait in
a passage, fired several shots to create panic and confusion. A roar of pain and rage rose up on all sides. Street
vendors hurriedly packed up their junk, caught up in an
indescribable hubbub. Stalls were crushed, others abandoned. Among the rebels, the police and the armed
gangs it was impossible to tell who was spilling out of the
nearby streets. Wails, cries, shouts were rising from the
crowd. With a determination I didn't know I had, I
elbowed myself a route through this flood of people
spilling out onto the pavements. A moment later, Lolo
grabbed hold of my blouse. And the crowd swept me
along with her to the door of a clinic on Rue Capois. The
shots were gaining in intensity. I stumbled against a body
and stopped myself from falling by clinging on to a tele-
graph pole. A student, mortally wounded, stared at me,
eyes rolling. The man who had killed him was standing
right in front of me. In rags, wild to the core, he was
hardly sixteen years old: with no past, with no future,
with no relatives, nature stripped bare, a bloody wound
rubbed raw. He stared at me unblinking with an icy
irony. It was a great effort to stop myself from throwing
up my breakfast. Three women rushed down a passage-
way, bumping into me as they passed. I felt a heavy
panic take me over. I turned and had lost sight of Lolo.
A hand seized me by the collar and pulled me through a
gateway. And I clearly heard a man's voice.

'Come on.'

THIRTEEN

I go down the aisle again, comforting the sick, administering drops, distributing tablets, ordering the auxiliaries to change dressings. On the right is the young woman who gave birth yesterday and whose baby is sharing the narrow bed. Since the mysterious disappearance of a baby girl three months ago, mothers have not wanted to be apart from their newborns. The administration has not insisted and has even been rubbing its hands in glee at the idea of staff reductions and fewer expenses. There is nothing left of the crèche but a name, the mattresses and the few remaining chairs that have not been stolen and are simply waiting for the vandals, who will also have been considering the fastest way to remove the cots, to finish the job. On the left I stop to take hold of the gnarled fingers of an old woman who is dying and try in vain to guess what her eyes are trying to tell me from behind the milky veil of a cataract. And then there is the strong, silent man. A man in his forties. Two beds down from the old woman. He arrived the previous week while I was on night duty, looming up suddenly like an apparition. Everything about him was of the night – his eyes, his courage, his silence. The effect was so striking that you couldn't help but look at him, even in his pain. He replied to my questions without apparent distrust, but I knew that, deep inside, he was distrustful. As we all are. On this island we are made that way. It is a game to which we devote the brightest of our days, a result of living within reach of those whom we have good reason to distrust. Suffice to say that I know little more about this man than that his stomach ulcer had bled for the first time the day before he arrived in this hospital.

It is already a year since Fignolé left this same hospital, and cried out to me as he arrived back in Mother's and Joyeuse's room, 'I will never go back within those walls, Angélique, you understand? Never!'

He went on to say that he would prefer to die at home or in the street like a beggar, like a stray dog, rather than stay one second longer within the walls of this hospital. That what he feared most was not so much dying as waking up in this white prison. Of experiencing the implacable return of the morning's horrors, surrounded by twenty or so others who nursed the same fears deep inside. He said all this as he talked to Joyeuse, who put her arms round his shoulders and hugged him close. Sitting on Mother's big bed, they were unaware of my presence. They didn't even notice how they were tormenting me, wounding me with their whispered confidences, their embraces, their tears, like two young cats would worry a bird. The idea of holding Fignolé's hands in mine suggested itself for a few seconds, a moment during which I felt their claws scratch a few words of wounded love into my skin. A moment in which I straightened my skirt and adjusted the neck of my blouse.

I then left the room with silent steps, creeping down the passage like a creature of the night.

I will soon breeze down to the end of the ward, past the two young boys injured by bullets. The first with damage to his collarbone and neck; the second, the younger of the two, with a pierced abdomen and bladder. They were brought here at daybreak. The youngest will die soon; it's a matter of hours. He has lost too much blood. The other will come through it. But I won't tell them. When she arrived early this morning, the youth's mother slipped a rosary between his fingers and placed a scapular round his neck. As I approach, the youth raises a face with features distorted by pain and stupor. The stupor of one who is holding on and finds himself face to face with the ineffable. I give him a smile, as best I can. All these young men remind me of Fignolé.

Fignolé, who has never accepted the rules of any dogma, any uniform, any doctrine. Who at a very early stage began to wrestle with that which we call reality, without really knowing what it entails. And who lived in self-imposed exile in a solitude we believed to be radiant but from where he showed himself to be powerless against the setbacks of the world. Fignolé, who was incapable of becoming part of this life, of following its movements, its hours, minutes and seconds. Fignolé, incapable of growing up overtaken by a fast-flowing flood, preferring to sink. Fignolé now drags behind him a despair that burns his blood. The first trigger was without doubt the arrest of Uncle Octave.

I remember that incident, at which Fignolé was present, as if it were yesterday. The presidency of the son of the other Prophet-President, President for Life, was coming to an end. It was days before Fignolé was able to tell us about it, his voice a monotone. From the day of that incident on, he was never the same. Mother simply said to me one day: 'Fignolé will burn himself out, char his flesh to the bone. And it will be one of us, if not all three of us, who will be forced to sweep up his ashes.'

He told us that a car came to a stop outside Octave's house. Octave's only crime was to be the assistant accountant for a paper no-one was supposed to write for and no-one was supposed to read. The incident took place in the district of Gressier to the south of Port-au-Prince. Fignolé was barely thirteen. He and Octave's two sons immediately recognised Merisié, his high forehead and figure slender as a cane. A kind of legendary ogre whom many could describe but only a few knew. Great powers were attributed to him, and a capacity for inflicting extraordinary tortures. He started as a Tonton Macoute at Fort-Dimanche, the Dungeon of Death with the former Prophet, the President for Life. Some people swear by what they hold most precious that Merisié can turn himself into a cat, disappear or make himself immune to bullets, even those fired from point-blank range. Merisié was accompanied by Gwo Louis. It was the latter who deliberately made the tyres of the car crunch noisily on the gravel in the street.

Gwo Louis was Merisié's bodyguard, an armoured regiment on two legs at the exclusive service of his boss. Ex-militia man Merisié had succeeded in surviving another Prophet-President for Life, with round spectacles and a black fedora. Part civil servant, part spy, Merisié was a grand master of base deeds. But just as there is no end to the servility of people on this island, so Gwo Louis was the grand master of deeds even more base than those of Merisié. The absolute low of the low. Gwo Louis, who had a chest substantially broader than the average, leaned his face out of the window, displaying his head for the three youths to admire. A head so big you could imagine it was sculpted from rock. Behind this face you could make out a terrifying reptilian venom, and beneath the thick layer of fat the power of a wildcat. And, of course, a great, boundless stupidity.

Eyes on fire like two beasts of the Apocalypse, they got out of the car and with their guns on display slammed the doors and advanced towards the boys. Merisié began by pacing up and down, hands behind his back, fixing each of the boys in turn with his stare. From the outset, Merisié accused them of wanting to threaten the safety of peaceable citizens at the instigation of Octave. From wanting to disturb the peace of the neighbourhood to a crime against the security of the State was a small step, which Merisié made in the following seconds, treating the boys as trouble-makers, opponents of an established government. He threatened to cut them up into pieces.

To break their bones.

To slit their throats.

To smash into their chests and gouge out their hearts.

To open up their stomachs and drag out their guts and intestines.

As for their genitals, their penises and testicles, he promised them with a gnashing of teeth that he would season them with salt and paprika and eat them with rice and kidney beans.

Standing at the entrance to the tiny gallery, Gwo Louis deterred them from any idea of running away. He punctuated Merisié's demented speech with a noisy, vulgar laugh which shook his fat bulk. To the great surprise of his cousins, Fignolé moved towards Merisié and asked him why he was angry. His sole reply was to tell Fignolé in no uncertain terms that he'd be the first to be cut into pieces. And he mimed taking aim at them one by one as they did in cops-and-gangster films on the TV. Uncle Octave, who was visiting a neighbour, was alerted and ran back to his house. When Uncle Octave arrived, Merisié gave a sign to Gwo Louis, who shoved into him, then immobilised him by twisting his hands up behind his back. Octave was taken away by these two men and we never saw him again.

Fignolé, pure metal. Someone who has always wanted to think for himself. Who believes that freedom is not first and foremost a right, but a duty, a demand. Jean-Baptiste and Wiston did not understand him. Even John, armed with all his qualifications, could not, would not follow him. Could not understand that in the name of this freedom he had turned against the head of the Démunis after his return to power and joined the new wave of insurrection on the streets. The last argument between them had been violent. Fignolé did not hesitate to shout out his anger at John, to tell him what he thought of him, an aristocrat from the well-to-do neighbourhoods of Philadelphia come to warm up his soul in the tropics. Come to dispel his rich kid's boredom by sowing chaos among the poor whom he admired like exotic animals walking around on their hind legs. And because of this abrupt change in Fignolé, in the film he played in his head, John had to find himself a new role. We never saw him again in our house. His absence left me neither cold nor warm. It is so easy for someone like John to be nice and good and to invent stories for books and films. John has a future. We don't. There are rich people, others are poor. We will always be poor, John always rich. John is not one of our own and never will be.

I turn before leaving the large ward and catch the surprised gaze of the stranger seizing mine like a pair of hands. God protect me from the expression of this man who wants nothing so much as to awake in me the greatest possible terror and take delight in doing so. Like those strangers on the look-out along the roadsides.

God protect me from the eyes of this man who could send me headlong into Hell.

FOURTEEN

I was literally grabbed by this unknown hand, and shoved so forcefully that I lost my balance, stumbling on the broken surface of a short, narrow alleyway leading to a wooden door protected by a grille. As I came up before this door I suddenly remembered Lolo, whom I had lost in the crowd. As the idea came to me that something could have happened to her, my panic gave way to a turmoil that I could barely contain. I yelled at this man who had just saved my life that I had a friend who was still outside and that she could perhaps be dead as we spoke. The man begged me to calm down and told me he would take me to a safe place first and then go out to look for her.

My saviour, who I could now see properly for the first time, knocked on the door three times with his left hand. I moved my eyes to his right hand, which was still holding me. It was covered in blood. This was the first image I had of him, the hand and the blood. The smell, slightly acrid, of the blood came to me as I bent down to refasten a sandal strap that had come loose and my right cheek brushed against his fingers. He crouched down. I raised my head and saw his face right next to mine. Close up, like at the cinema. An image that erased all the others and would later take its place next to that of his whole body. And then, the voice.

'Open up, it's me.'

The door opened a little. A young man, thinner than my saviour, first of all showed his face obliquely behind the half-open door and then moved to stand, visibly surprised, before us.

'I've brought you a guest. Take care of her and wait while I go and look for another.'

My saviour grabbed a piece of fabric that was lying on a table and wrapped it round his hand. As his friend continued to stare in amazement, my saviour added with a smile:

'I'll explain later.'

I looked at that face again. Listened to the voice. The face was finely sculpted, manly, attractive. The voice had a slight edge. There was a hint of trouble in that voice that cracked now and again, making you want to smooth the edges. A voice that formed a wall you wanted to break through. A voice that even then stirred my senses and my blood.

My saviour took to the alleyway again and disappeared behind the barrier across the entrance. The crackling of gunfire began to recede. Then, little by little, the noises from outside vanished. A deathly silence reigned over the city, a silence more terrifying than the tumult. The time that separated me from the return of Lolo and my saviour seemed even more interminable. Anxious, I couldn't keep still; I sat down, stood up, paced up and down, then slumped into a chair opposite the youth who had stayed with me in the house. But it was more than the mere fear of death or injury. I couldn't explain that spasm in my chest, that knot that was slowly tightening, that lump in my throat.

When I heard a knocking on the door I rushed to open it immediately. The youth halted me with a gesture, signalled to me to hurry away towards the back door and placed his index finger across his lips to indicate that I should be quiet and not move. He stood on a chair against the wall and looked through a hole above the door. My saviour knocked impatiently a second time.

'It's me, open up!'

I could already hear Lolo sobbing and moaning. The youth who stayed with me hurried to open the door and in his haste knocked over the chair, which in turn tripped me up. Lolo erupted through the open door like a volcano and threw herself into my arms. Pleased as she was that she had not been hit by a bullet, she was inconsolable about the idea of having lost her first mobile phone. She cried hot tears, and as I comforted her I couldn't help thinking that Lolo, with her fertile imagination, was constructing in her head a Hollywood film where she played the role of victim simultaneously with that of some Mother Courage, which she would show in a mass of detail before spellbound audiences. Once I was able to raise my head, I saw my saviour talking to the other youth with a serious air. He was standing, backlit, in the doorway, his silhouette superimposed against the noon sky. I tried to catch snatches of their conversation, without realising that I was already under the spell of this man. God, how I wanted to close my eyes and stretch myself against him! How I wanted it! When he turned, his eyes met mine and his laugh burst out like a guava beneath the pressure of a hand.

Outside, the commotion had gone completely quiet. Taking advantage of the general calm, the other youth suggested we share two bottles of pop, bread and grapefruit jelly.

'It's all we have,' he said. And he introduced himself. I heard that he was called Evans and he lived on the ground floor with his mother. That Luckson, whom he indicated with his hand, had joined him when his mother, a Madame Sarah, went off on business to Curaçao. That they were both studying mathematics at university. On hearing these words, Lolo threw me a sidelong glance. I pretended I hadn't seen her, as I knew what she meant.

Luckson simply acknowledged us with a movement of his head, sank his teeth into a piece of bread and sat down on the ground, making light of the injury to his hand. I still love this image of him. Sitting with his knees bent under him, his torso half naked, his head inclined. All I have to do is go back over those few weeks to be fully immersed in these images. Again and again.

Always quick to assess and take advantage of a situation involving the opposite sex, Lolo quickly introduced us.

'I'm Marie-Lourdes, Lolo to those who know me, and my friend is Joyeuse.'

I finished my drink quickly and replied with a trite, meaningless comment. I then thanked them and said we should be getting back. They reminded us that we could not yet be sure that the streets were safe. The Sacré-Coeur clock was striking three by the time we left them. There were no longer any clouds of black smoke from burning tyres drifting up from the four corners of the city. Fear was spreading its wings more insidiously. Furtive shapes slipped along the walls. We crossed deserted streets as if on the outskirts of a dream. And I thought of your face, Luckson, your mouth and your face. And already I wanted to taste it. To touch you. I wanted you to be mine. The whole world could vanish leaving just you and me.

Seeing me arrive home, Fignolé stopped strumming his guitar and looked at me.

'What's happened to you? You look all shaken up. What's with that blood on your T-shirt?'

'I'm not hurt, don't worry. I was caught up in the incidents at the top of Rue Pavée. Someone helped Lolo and me.'

'That's all, you're sure?'

Something must have been written all over my face, giving me away.

'What else do you want there to be? I could ask you the same thing. You're lathered in sweat. Where have you been to get like that?'

'You know perfectly well. So don't ask questions. You'll risk upsetting Mother.'

Without explaining any more, he simply took off his T-shirt, picked up his guitar and played the first notes of Redemption Song by Bob Marley, his favourite music.

> *Redemption song*
> *Emancipate yourselves*
> *From mental slavery*

Listening to the news the next day I understood that he had followed at arm's length those who were carrying the coffin of young Maxime, circling the city centre. The journalist's words on that day still resonate with me: 'Students hostile to the Prophet-President insisted on accompanying the body of Maxime as far as the southern exit from the city towards Martissant... Everything went tragically wrong when several hundred of them came up to the railings outside the National Palace... Some demonstrators were injured when stones were thrown by the Prophet-President's supporters. Later on, four of them were wounded by bullets and another shot while they were trying to run away towards Rue Capois.'

These events happened exactly one month ago. I had just met Luckson, a strong-willed man, a man of love. This meeting did nothing to uproot the certainty I feel that Fignolé is gambling with his life.

FIFTEEN

In the cafeteria there is a pervasive smell of medicines and blood. And if there is anyone who thinks that we are not surrounded on all sides, all they need to do is to sit by the windows for the smell of fried fish and rancid oil, the powerful taint of rubbish, to persuade them to the contrary.

Port-au-Prince, the outpost of despair. Port-au-Prince, a great settlement of concrete and mud on a grassy plain. Port-au-Prince, my torment and my punishment. All these images, all this past history. Two centuries of secret misdeeds inscribed in the walls. The city's descent into Hell began too long ago for me to complain about it. As for the absence of Fignolé, I'm not complaining about that, either. I phone Madame Jacques. She sends for Mother, who tells me that Paulo has gone to look for news around Martissant and has not yet returned. After a few seconds she adds in a voice she is trying to make seem firmer than necessary, 'If Fignolé still isn't back by the time you get home you should go and tell the police.'

Mother's words leave my mind blank for a moment, as if I have lost the true meaning of things. I recover myself by thinking of the word of God, which I repeat, eyes closed:

> *God is powerful*
> *The horse and his rider he has thrown into the sea*
> *God has become my salvation.*

Gabriel goes with me to the Pentecostal church every Sunday, sometimes on the Tuesday fast days. There, I meet the faithful, crowded together on the narrow pews. Between the four walls of the church, we delight in the words that Pastor Jeantilus rains down on us from his pulpits. The beauty and poetic extravagance of all these tales enter our hearts, surprising us every time: Lazarus rising from the tomb, Jonah emerging from the belly of the whale, the walls of Jericho collapsing at the sound of the trumpets, the abundant fishing of Jesus, Jesus himself walking on water! Pastor Jeantilus croons and is enchanted by the resonance of his own voice. He moves us and wrings us out every Sunday like the purple seaweed riding the foam. Pastor Jeantilus, a real magician!

I have brought Gabriel up to fear God. To be horrified by sin. A far cry from the lightness of Joyeuse, the mischief of Fignolé. From the superstitions of Mother. Nourished from birth on the word of the prophets and the psalms of David, in this little church where men, women and children gather, hands joined, mouths open, singing and chanting. Sometimes Brother Derrick, a big American evangelist, comes from his native Kansas to preach to us with zeal. In his dark three-piece suit, Pastor Jeantilus gets so agitated behind his lectern that he works up large beads of sweat. Sister Yvette, his wife, follows him, a towel in her hand, and wipes his face. Pastor Jeantilus, his eyes closed, his whole body trembling, always finishes by summoning in his cavernous voice the angels of Heaven and the demons of Hell who in their turn take possession of the faithful or depart their bodies. A finger pointed to Heaven, he fixes us with his eyes and petrifies us. From his pulpit, like from a mountain-top, he breathes out the word of God from the depths of his lungs. He is like the wind rushing through the depths of a forest, moving the tops of the trees and shaking the crazy branches. Eyes closed, spirit reaching out, he imposes his voice and his force on this vale of humanity. And as he speaks we cry out 'Amen' and 'Your name be blessed, Lord Jesus'. And we wave our arms from side to side. 'Alleluia! Alleluia!'

Only last Sunday a man who was there, battered, visibly exhausted, shouted out while waving his arms that he was waiting for the firm touch of God's work. Her body shaken by convulsions, her eyes rolling, a woman wept the tears of Niobe. Through her tears she cited all the want, the deprivation, the hunger of her world. Manette, a frail young girl recently come to live in our neighbourhood, confessed her acquaintance with the devil and cried out at the top of her voice her desire to renounce Satan, his pomp and his works. She told of what she alone had seen, things capable of appalling people and driving them away from her for good. That great shadow of a hairy, horned figure stood before her, face gleaming, broad chest heaving and panting. Her eyes rolled up, she lifted the sleeve of her blouse and revealed the scar that this creature of darkness had scored onto her shoulder with the fine point of a knife. This testimony caused the faithful, squeezed tightly together, to cry out their faith at the tops of their voices until the walls of the building shook. Other miracles are produced before our eyes, day after day. Pastor Jeantilus has built up the church and has recently begun to arrive to bring us the message of God in a brand-new car. God indeed moves in mysterious ways!

Standing at my side, Gabriel has listened to all these extraordinary words. Nourished by the words of the prophets and the apostles, Gabriel has sung and prayed. I can still see him, wide-eyed, heart beating, turned towards Pastor Jeantilus, this speaker of spells, this teller of marvels.

All these stories have not, however, prevented Gabriel from asking me, exactly a fortnight ago, who his father was. Without the slightest hesitation, my nose once again rubbed into my sin, I replied that he had died shortly after his birth. However false this notion, I wanted it to be the foundation on which Gabriel builds his life from now on. Between him and the nothingness from which he emerged, between him and eternity, there will be this lie. The words seemed as if they were coming from the mouth of a stranger, one of those who inhabit me. Those for whom I have never known how to make space, and who appear suddenly with hardly a sound. And that is why my reply vanished as anger and remorse grabbed me by the throat.

SIXTEEN

These disturbing memories that assail me make the tap-tap journey to the uptown commercial district seem much shorter than usual. After getting off the vehicle I go to a public phone box and again call the mysterious number written by Fignolé on that scrap of paper. Without success. I get the voicemail service again. And once again, I don't leave a message.

I walk through the streets of the city centre which breathe to the rhythm of its strangely calm crowds. How long will they remain calm? No-one can say. The city centre also has its mysteries. Working in this luxury shop, I have come to understand that its upper echelons, distributed in an enigmatic order, include German and French descendants and immigrants from the Middle East. Mixed blood, great-grandchildren and grandchildren of the natural sons of a fornicating, arrogant conqueror, bent on dissipating the remains of African blood or adapting to it as they would adapt to rather disreputable family secrets. Everyone has their history. More or less glorious, more or less acceptable, hints of which I have caught in snatches of conversations picked up from Madame Herbruch, my boss. Reported words. Rumours placed end to end, that I associate with certain faces, unknown to them. The pieces of a jigsaw, the whole of which is totally insipid, mediocre, hollow.

I open the doors of the shop mechanically, caught in a pincer movement between these thoughts and my anxiety at the absence of Fignolé. As she does every morning,

Yanick Lahens

the vendor sitting by the entrance offers me seasonal fruits, mangos, soursops, cachimans or pomegranates. Every day Madame Herbruch drives her away, her and the others who crowd round the door. And every day they make a show of shifting a few metres up or down the street, then gradually creep back those few metres they have moved in one direction or another, to return to the same place.

'Too expensive,' I retort to the fruit seller. She must have mistaken me for someone else. The poor do not buy fruit. Or very rarely. We pick them from the trees or we pinch them. But she sees fit to insist. This little game has been going on between us for several months. I know she will get me in the end by wearing me down. Wearing down – the most formidable weapon there is, as I know from trying it myself with Madame Herbruch herself and those before whom I should resist or disappear. The fruit seller in turn tries it on Madame Herbruch and me. We therefore wear one another down to the bone, to the marrow.

I will never forget the day when Madame Herbruch asked me to help her with a large banquet she was preparing in her luxurious residence. When I crossed the living room to the beautiful toilet with its blue ceramics beneath the stairs, I felt the eyes of the prestigious guests burn into me, reducing me to the mere idea of a being. To these bourgeois mulattoes with their fair skin I was not a budding young woman but merely a black female of a breed with simple, distinctive equipment: two breasts and a vagina. A breed doomed to the shanties, to domestic service, or to bed.

After closing the toilet door, I leant against it to catch my breath and give a moment's freedom to my feet that were suffering in too-tight shoes. It is events like this that penetrate a life like a violent torrent that slashes through dry, hard earth.

84

On the wall across from me hung a reproduction of an autumn scene. To this day I do not know why this picture had such an effect on me. I had never seen the autumn, but school books and the television had given me a glimpse of the beauty of leaves in this season, colours that set the trees ablaze. It was a scene from elsewhere, a landscape from elsewhere. People from elsewhere. In what must have been the garden of a manorhouse, two little girls with blonde hair were playing, laughing, watched lovingly by their parents. I told myself this must be the image of happiness, of paradise, this impression of tranquil abundance, of carefree serenity. The promise of a life without hardships, without cares, without needs. Recalling my geography lessons, I imagined the list of countries that might be home to such a scene and after hesitating between the English, Danish and German countryside I settled on the Danish countryside, as I thought it was the furthest removed from this place where chance had decreed I should be born. This image has never left me.

Madame Herbruch phones me as I arrive to reassure herself that I have made the journey despite the barricades that have been blazing since the dawn. She reminds me to ensure that the cleaning lady wipes the shelves and to make certain there is coffee and a jar of guava jam, her favourite, in case she calls by in the early afternoon.

I am prepared to accept anything from Madame Herbruch. Madame Herbruch is a springboard. Madame Herbruch already belongs to my past. Sitting at the table, I take out the notebook containing the notes from my business studies course. But I won't be reading a line of it today. I am waiting for a brother who likes to play with fire, who plays reason off against insanity. A brother of sun and lightning. Inside me there is something greater than I am, planted by Luckson, a man whom I hardly know and who turns my soul inside out like a glove.

SEVENTEEN

Gabriel was born of a treacherous act by one of those many men of immediate pleasure and no tomorrow. One of those men who wear the male mask of boastfulness and unconcern and whom I didn't recognise for what he was until too late. It was the time before I discovered the word of God. Before the Redemption. Before Pastor Jeantilus. Now, from daybreak until the moment when the dark of the night envelops me, I turn the same question over and over in my head: who is this man, Gabriel's father? I wait for the moment when I can wash away the stain of my mistake. I wait for this past that hammers at my ears to fall silent.

I recall the light of an afternoon, a walk by the sea that I was discovering for the first time. Perhaps, in all this story, account should be taken of the sun and the sea. Of my delight in this white-hot day. The blue of the water. The dazzling light. My spirit filled with wonder at such extravagance and beauty. Such splendour given, offered – without a fight, without sacrifice. Such a profusion of splendour. So many sparkling images. Light dancing on the foam and waves coming to lap at my ankles. I keep this memory, a blend of soursop and pomegranate. Enough to make your skin prickle with the feet of crazy ants. To make you forget the name of your mother or your country. A kind of inebriation seizing hold of me. A mouth on mine. Tongues entwining. Silent kisses. Murmurs and promises. A body against mine. A hand on my breasts. My body split in two. And the world swaying around me...

The scarcest glimpse of pleasure, trousers zipped up. A handkerchief to wipe away a few white drops, a pinkish streak, left on my stomach. Between my thighs. Sticking to my fingers. Then very soon, becoming a blemish that I washed away every day like a child dirtied by mud and games. I had a desire to slash my lips so that no man could place his own lying, deceitful mouth there. To mutilate my genitals so they would no longer be of use to these conquerors so full of haughty pride. And then there was my stomach, more swollen day by day as the fruit grew inside. Every day my body felt the disaster. Mirrors kept giving me the image of my decomposition. I had this shame that made a dull noise inside my head, that gnawed at my guts, that I still try to curb to this day like a wild horse so that I can get out of bed and put one foot in front of the other some mornings.

I wait for the curse to be lifted, for the bad spell to be cleared! I wait...

Like me, Mother didn't know that she was carrying a child. She confided it to me a few years ago, one day when I was surrounding her with questions:

'One morning I felt bad, but I didn't immediately make the link between what the man, your father, had done and this sickness that was unfamiliar to me. It was my mother who told me, when, the next day and the next, I threw up everything I had ingested since birth. Mother made me lie down on my bed, looked at me, and as two tears slid down her cheeks, she caressed me to reassure me. The man disappeared. Took off. Without leaving the slightest trace.'

As for me, from the start I wanted this child out of me. There were moments when I thought I was going to die. The smell of herring, that of armpits, of frying, of cheap Sunday perfumes, all filled my nostrils, penetrated my stomach only to come back out of my mouth in nauseous waves. And I wanted to do everything a woman does when she wants to get rid of a child. To go to an unknown woman who would make me drink a greenish liquid and would leave me for three whole days in a chasm of pain until I expelled from my belly that thing that had become attached there despite myself. It was not Mother's words that made me change my mind, but Joyeuse, my little fairy at that time, who never stopped stroking my stomach once she knew that a little red oyster had made its nest there. She would often place her cheek on it, close her eyes and remain there for a long moment of contemplation...

At the table next to mine, the other nurses are chatting away nineteen to the dozen. Darline, who I don't like and who feels the same towards me, is animatedly giving out the details of the festive atmosphere last Sunday at the Champ de Mars as the carnival approached. A young DJ set the place alight by pouring out the best merengues of the carnival from the speakers. Unable to hold back a moment longer, Darline rises from her seat as the others laugh, to demonstrate how she had swayed her hips, moving her buttocks in all directions like a top. She doesn't stop looking over towards me, to be sure that her poisoned arrows have hit home. But it doesn't work. These girls are possessed... I know it. Possessed... I humbly ask God to spare them from all the diseases lying in wait, and to lead them, Darline and the others, to repent. Burying my nose in my plastic bowl I eat with complete indifference yesterday's rice with a single meatball that I have brought from home.

From nowhere, suddenly and despite myself, I think of the stranger who arrived a few days ago. The stranger lying in the big ward never complains. Rarely speaks. And when he does his words are few. But I can sense a strength that moves in silence beneath his skin, his muscles, his torso. This man seems capable of resisting everything – the bite of the sun, the fury of the waters, the provocations of a woman. My own involuntary provocation as I prepared to give him an injection three days ago and our heads touched above his bed.

You have hurt me, my friend, with a single hair from the back of your neck.

The contact of his skin on mine had the effect on me of a static electric shock. And his eyes were fixed on the swell of my breasts. I was ashamed of what I felt – I, Angélique Méracin, practising Christian. Perhaps he takes me for something I am not, a female on heat. And not for what I am, a poor woman beseeching God for assistance. A poor woman tempted by the Devil. I crucified myself by that very task on that day, waiting for the evening service and the following Tuesday's fast.

I look through the window at the unbroken blue of the sky. The blue of a false paradise. But so beautiful… So beautiful. I would like there to be a sun inside me that is as perfect as this blue. Perhaps it would mean that I can erase the conqueror, forget that strong man. Forget that I am waiting for Fignolé. I who have not discovered how to bridge the distance Fignolé has placed between himself and the world. I who have not discovered, in that marsh I wade through, anything other than tedium. A life gnawed at by the worms of tedium.

Bursting into my thoughts as if breaking chains, a young auxiliary arrives at a run: 'The young wounded man has gone delirious.'

Of course I haven't finished my lunch. I leave the bowl and the plate as they are and run towards the big ward.

EIGHTEEN

Fignolé always had the face of a child who was different. One of those children of the light whom the
shadows observe and around whom madness and death
prowl. Very early on I wanted to confront those shadows
for him. Very early on I wanted to be his rampart against
death. And I took this part upon myself, devoting myself
to the all-important occupation of keeping him on his
feet. Safe and sound. Whatever the cost, whichever way
the wind blew.

As children, Fignolé and I played all kinds of games.
When Fignolé dressed up my old rag doll, Mother
shouted from inside the house that he would do better to
run after a ball. When I ran after the ball with him,
Mother warned me against the misfortunes that only
boys could bring me. We laughed up our sleeves, or
sometimes so loudly that the earth of the cramped back
yard seemed to burst apart on the spot and rise up in
eddying dust clouds. We ran, tasting the luminous air of
the Tropics. Fignolé is my soulmate, a reflection of
myself, my brother in love. Our bodies are still those of
the angels of our childhood.

I recall the east-facing paving stone in front of the
house that often stayed cool into the afternoon. I was
lying on my stomach on this cold paving stone, topless.
Fignolé was at my side. Our bodies had been covered
with a mixture of starch and kleren, an infallible remedy
against heat bumps. But the heat always ended up getting the better of us. Fignolé had his head on my chest

and we were both dozing – a moment I wish had never ended. I awoke abruptly and watched him sleeping. And I guarded him for two whole hours against all the dangers of the world that could arrive in succession to threaten him: floods, the injustice of adults, illnesses, cyclones, dog bites and whatever else.

You alone, Fignolé, have the power to take the place of my whole childhood. You alone were able to extinguish before time the pleasures of my childhood. And feelings of astonishment and amazement, terror and pride would rise up in me all at once to see you when you were smaller, weaker and soon to become wilder. An extraordinary love was to grow between us. A sacred union.

And then, little by little, I stopped seeing life as a group of clear lines beneath a big sun. I turned resolutely towards death to see it charging right at Fignolé. Right at me. At full speed like a huge dumper truck. And then, reaching an age of reason, I began to doubt the kindness of a God who could launch such a meteor at defenceless beings. I now thought it a matter of urgency, before this meteor struck us at full force, to classify everything in the world into the things which were important and those which were not. The important things included Fignolé, my brother, my son, my gift. And there was me.

Three years before Fignolé was born, Mother slapped away the man whom I see rarely, whose mistress she had been for a while and who is none other than my father. She courageously sought to support us in life, the three of us – Angélique, herself and me. She mended clothes, prepared pots of jam and made several return journeys to the Dominican Republic to sell cheap trinkets. A few dollars from Uncle Thémosthène, who had moved to Little Haiti, Miami, made it easier to make ends meet at the end of the month. And then one evening, against all expectations, Onil Hermantin, a man who, from time to time, had offered her consolation against the tribulations of ordinary life, asked her to marry him. To the great surprise of everyone, she accepted. She let down her guard before a man who was offering her a roof over her head and a ring on her finger. She was mistaken. But tell me, what woman, however strong she may be, would not want to be consoled once in her life? Tell me. This arrangement did not last long enough to leave its mark on her, but enough to sicken her like the smell of rotten fruit. A few months after the birth of Fignolé, Mother recovered her status of free woman with a relief she did not try to conceal. Mother had a husband and many lovers, but no man ever possessed her. None of them was her lord or master. They hardly shared their fleeting relief. They did not teach her much but a few techniques in bed. Gave her nothing but a few dollars. Mother is not one to buy the peace of a home by selling her soul.

She left the house, taking with her a little money, enough to keep herself for barely four days, the two bags containing our clothes, her three children and inside herself the certainty that she was coming out on top. Aunt Sylvanie helped us to move into a single room, damp and dark, at the end of a seedy passage. We three children all slept on a mattress on the floor behind a curtain cut from coarse cloth. It may have been only a room, but Mother wanted wherever she lived to be her own; she would not be accountable to anyone. At that time, when Mother offered food to the loas it was often Erzulie Fréda, Erzulie the beautiful, Erzulie the tender, who would possess her. After demanding all, the spirit would leave her lascivious and reassured.

One day, between moon and sun, when we had not eaten all day, a shadow appeared behind the drawn curtain. I let out a cry of fright. I was at that age where I still believed in creatures lying dormant in the legends or awaiting us in our dreams. Holding her nightshirt over her breasts, Mother placed her lips on my brow and whispered that one of them had come to visit us. I soon believed them capable of a thousand wonders as we ate better during the days following their furtive visits.

Without having to dress in revealing clothes, without swinging her hips, sometimes without having to make the slightest gesture, Mother could attract men. She was surrounded by a perfume of eroticism, of which she herself was not aware. She exuded sex like other women exude boredom. There were lovers who, some days, would listen to her talking before delighting her body. I always saw her make these men feel as if they were unique, and they believed her. And the light she radiated held them fast without them being able to do much to get free. Once under her spell, they were caught. There was no-one like her for drawing out the simplest words and giving them music, mellowness or resonance. I never heard a woman ask a man 'Will you have a coffee or a finger of rum?' with such sweetness. Mother had no idea of this sweetness that flowed from the depths of her wide eyes, from her voice of caves and expansive distances that constantly exhorted them to follow, from her violet, flower-like lips. She had no idea of the subtle invitation of her ample hips. However often I have delved into the metal box and taken out the yellowing, ageing photo that has fixed her at twenty-five, I still have not found the key to this mystery... Right now I suspect Maître Fortuné is ready to lay his cheek against her breasts and to kiss the hem of her dress.

Madame Thomas, the first customer, arrives around eleven o'clock, an hour after the shop opened. I hate Madame Thomas. A woman with an extravagant hairdo dyed in tawny shades, with outrageous make-up, having applied every artifice. Madame Thomas belongs to the nouveau riche set who give the city a flashy gaiety in total contrast to the hordes of destitutes who are still in the process of encircling it.

'Joyeuse, bring me Madame Herbruch's new stock to look at.'

'Of course,' I reply with a smile that doubtless does little to conceal my irritation.

Madame Thomas inspects the whole of the dress section, the accessories and the shelf of shoes. As usual she turns the shop upside down. I read in her eyes what her lips do not say: 'You can sulk and curse silently all you like, my girl; I don't care. I could buy the shop and you with it.'

But Madame Thomas is mistaken. She can't buy everything. This fine edifice of Madame Herbruch's conceals some major faults. Madame Thomas herself is worried. If I've understood correctly, her young gigolo by the name of James, fifteen years her junior, decided to drop her a week ago. The advice of Madame Herbruch no longer makes any difference. I assume that young James prefers to satisfy himself, alone and whenever the fancy takes him, beneath the eyes of God, rather than awake a dead soul. Fignolé always made clear his aversion for her starchy type, and for that other type, imbued with arrogance, the privileged of any age. Fignolé told me on one of his talkative days that something was there turning the world against us and all those like us. That life was an absurd lottery where those who won have everything and those who lost, nothing. Absolutely nothing. Madame Thomas, for the moment, is visibly savouring her gains.

'You're right, Fignolé, the world is divided between the dogs and those who hit them on their muzzles. Joyeuse does not want to hit anyone, Fignolé, but has sworn not to be on the side of the dogs.'

I grit my teeth, hold my tongue firmly and think of my pay at the end of the month. A salary that doesn't bring in much. A salary without fanfare but that I can't turn my nose up at. And I dream of the day when I, too, can go to a luxury shop and, forgetting everything, have the shelves emptied for me one by one by an ill-tempered assistant. Actually, I don't dream. I hone my weapons. I sharpen my fangs. I have this force in me which knows how to confront the pain, reduce sorrow to silence. I care nothing for changing the world. I want to howl with the wolves.

NINETEEN

The skin of the wounded young man has taken on that greyish hue that is so familiar to me, and that foretells no good. The blood is not irrigating the arteries and the veins very well. And his moans are getting louder and louder. As he moans, a kind of foam comes from his mouth. The auxiliary fails to notice and I wipe the corners of his mouth with a little square of cloth given to me by his mother. The moment when I lift his head and move the cloth towards his lips, he loses control and shouts right out. I call the duty doctor as a matter of urgency.

The injured boy's mother is shaken by convulsions. It takes two assistant nurses to get her under control and lead her out for a moment. The moans of the youth then become louder than before. They no longer come from his throat, but are scraped out from deep in his belly, shorn of that last modesty to which he has been clinging. He cries without holding back at all. The sobs and moans of a young man of eighteen are more terrible than the Apocalypse. But the Apocalypse has already happened so many times on this ward, so many times in this city, on this island. And so many times the world has continued on its way, impassive.

The young patient finally collapses, taking on the glassy-eyed, lost expression of the dying. At the first question of the doctor, the young patient nevertheless shows him his left side. When the doctor bends gently over him to examine it, feeling with his fingers, the young man moans like a suffering beast. The doctor then takes an ampoule from the tray held by the auxiliary and gives him an injection, to stop the pain and the cries. During the preceding days, as the injection wore off he began to suffer and cried out again. This afternoon he is numb from suffering. Above all, he is afraid of dying. Between two groans, incomprehensible words emerge from his mouth, distorted by pain. His forehead is damp. Cold. Death will not be long. It is a question of minutes, of seconds.

It is hard to imagine the sun outside. Perhaps it is to reassure himself of its presence that the dying young man turns his head towards the only window of this ward from where you can see the sky. I look with him at this sky that he is without doubt seeing for the last time. It is desperately blue, pure as it often is in this season. The youth turns back to the other side of his bed. The side where his mother is. His eyelids gradually grow heavy and the gap between his moans increases until they die down, fading to a round of silence. I watch his sleep attentively, keeping a vigilant eye on him until his last breath. Until a death that comes without delay.

I use a cloth to bind the jaw of the young man who has just died, and place his hands together on his stomach. 'Until when will I still be driven by this undiminished desire to rub shoulders with death without batting an eyelid? Until when?' Every day I come up against it. Every day it brings me to sit on the edge of my own tomb. And every day I wake up in the same ignorance. However often I face the death of others, my own remains alien to me. I tell myself simply that a normal being could not leave the vicinity of their own tomb every day like I do, with all these scars and blemishes inside their own soul, and believe themselves unscathed. Impossible!

Passing close by the strong, silent man this afternoon,

I would like him to reach out an arm and stop me. I would like him to squeeze my hand tightly, passing on all the warmth his words evade. I would like him to say something, anything. I would even be able to bear his words dying in his throat, if only his expression would tell me he finds me strong and feminine. And for the first time since that afternoon on the shore, I feel a great emptiness deep down inside.

'What am I supposed to do with this body that suddenly feels so heavy, too heavy for me to bear alone?' I repeat to myself over and over again.

I pass through the hospital barrier almost at a run, my head as full as a jug. I breathe in the air on the street; it has never seemed so soothing. I undo another button on my blouse the better to fill my lungs with it.

TWENTY

Once Madame Thomas has left, I call the mysterious phone number again. Still in vain. I wait for a sign, watch for an apparition. Perhaps I am thinking about Fignolé more than I should. The tears rise from my heart to my eyes. I grasp onto my grey stone. The more hours that pass, the further away I am from a happy ending. Images take me over. All the same – black and terrible.

It is precisely half-past three. Time stands still, the hours fixed at mid-afternoon. Mother's words over the phone are hardly reassuring. On her return from Aunt Sylvanie's she kept the front door of the house ajar. Mother caught Wiston by surprise, obviously on guard as he slowed his pace to peer through the half-open door, and saved him some unnecessary contortions, as she put it: 'Wiston, there's no need to get a stiff neck; I'm here and Fignolé hasn't come home.' He gave a start and hurried away.

Mother's health has been getting worse for several weeks. Her knee troubles her mercilessly. Her dizzy spells happen more often and her ankles are swollen. She is worried about Fignolé but dares not say it. She attributes her complaints to the fact that Dambala, her master and her god, is not happy with her and feels neglected. Last year, because she had spent her money on Fignolé, Mother did not offer Dambala a ceremony worthy of his rank. And so she imagines he has remembered her, making her reel, her head heavier than a gourd full of water. When I told her I could do without gods who would take revenge on us poor creatures, she said, 'Hold your peace, my daughter, be quiet. You don't know what you're saying. You may not see God, Joyeuse, but the loas, you feel them right there in your body. They speak to you, they make you dance, get you money. They lay their hands on you, silence your cares, give you love, wipe away your tears. And when you're tired of waiting, you can make them face up to their responsibilities towards you and threaten them, saying things like: "Dambala, if I don't get this money within a month...". With them there is no cloud without a silver lining. No sin without forgiveness. No pain without healing. In this life of tribulation, of darkness and torment, the loas are your only morning dew, your only river of fresh water, your only window open to the sky.'

Unlike Angélique, Mother never expects anything of anyone. She responds to misfortune one step at a time, sometimes encircling it and embracing it. Angélique's life is a fruit of which she has eaten the best part without even noticing, without even tasting the juice. Those who get close to her sense in her a lukewarm indulgence that never leads to a deep, lasting relationship. Somewhere inside her she is marked with that sign that singles out the losers and ends up isolating them irreparably from the rest of humanity. Angélique has died that slow death that is the province of reprobates. Angélique has waited without getting that which she has been waiting for. Like many women, Angélique hoped for everything and, when it never came, lost it at a single stroke. Waiting for what you cannot have and realising too late that you will never have it makes for a life led in a narrow grind of sadness, the life of the defeated. Mother is exhausted but not defeated: 'Exhaustion bends your spine but defeat is ugly.' From the day when I first understood that something made the world turn against me and all those like me, I chose to become precisely the opposite of defeated, the opposite of exhausted.

I was not afraid when I arrived at the Sisters' up town. They would not admit to their school a little girl born out of wedlock, those whose intake was limited to the daughters of the middle classes, those from the good districts. A little bastard who had usurped the name of my Uncle Antoine, I broke my way into this world that was not mine. I was therefore already a substantial step ahead of the others. I already knew a whole world of things that they would never know. I knew want and deprivation. I knew absence, that of a father. And I had a foot in their universe. Of life, of death, I already had my personal view, fixed, one that had nothing to do with any catechism. The world I had grown up in until then was full of mistrust, treachery and danger. But I have not learned fear. I have not become cautious. The Sisters believed me gifted because I progressed through the levels year on year. I was not gifted, but curious, keen to understand how far those who had written the history of the world would go; those who, in their history, wanted me to be the worm they could crush beneath their heels. School did not give me the explanations I was expecting to all these questions; I found my responses to this mistrust, this treachery, this danger, by myself. To the extent that I don't remember crying as I read about the sufferings of Cosette. Nor did I feel any compassion for Cinderella, and later on, the watery misadventures of Manuel and Anaïs left me above all with a feeling of the greatest perplexity. As the years went by some girls saw my deficiencies as a kind of strangeness. They were wrong. They were wrong but I never told them. I never told them that all these deficiencies, all these deprivations, these dangers and these ruses had forged my capacity to survive, to live without love. Perhaps it was that love could have conquered me, and so I have always mistrusted love.

My boss arrives at two on the dot in her son Mike's luxury car. Mike has two main qualities. He has inherited from his father a Nordic physique in a land of Negroes who don't like themselves and a fortune in the midst of desolation that is too great to be fully counted. But Mike has already surpassed his father in cleverness. Since secondary school he has learned to cheat like his father, and since his misdeeds have now increased in scope and intensity, he has reached his late twenties with a small fortune that even his father can only dream about.

I am not well-placed to judge anyone, but the more the Herbruchs – father and son – steal, the more they accumulate and the more they whisper prayers into the ear of God, every Sunday and in full view of all. Monsieur Herbruch's negotiating skills have led him to come to terms even with the anger of God. Like his father, Mike will be the kind of man with a narrow imagination whose intelligence is limited to matters of business and who will do a lot of wrong, the kind of wrongs that are denounced every day on the radio and in certain papers that still believe in the power of the written or spoken word. I don't.

Madame Herbruch's parents experienced a change in fortunes. When a lack of money began to spread its smell of rottenness through the house they married my boss to Frantz Herbruch, that ungainly, conceited, soulless man. However, a few weeks later, Madame Herbruch, née Bérénice Pétillon, ended up finding him as handsome as Croesus. All the better for the fact that Frantz Herbruch turned out to be an undemanding lover who soon ceased to seek either a child or his own pleasure between her thighs. To remind each other of their own existence, from time to time they attack one another with bombshells of truths hatched from the lies of banal married life. Blood does not flow, but the effect is more or less the same.

Madame Herbruch has never found out that one afternoon of heavy rain, Monsieur Herbruch wanted to accompany me to the tap-tap station. Despite the rain I could hear his thoughts like the ticking of a clock and was hardly taken by surprise when, stopping the car, he placed one hand on my left breast and the other up my skirt. No doubt he was hoping to take me back to have a bit of fun in some bachelor pad and add me to his list of victims. I had known the appetites of men for a long time. Another before him, a respectable gentleman and a friend of Uncle Antoine, had already played the car trick on me. Staring directly into the eyes of Monsieur Herbruch, I reached down and impassively removed each of his hands before opening the car door and disappearing into the downpour. Ever since he has avoided my eye, but dare not have me sacked. Rest assured, Monsieur Herbruch, Joyeuse Méracin has other fish to fry.

I do not want to tell Madame Herbruch of my worries about Fignolé. I simply complete the day's accounts and ask her permission to leave early. In any case she knows I'm not there for ever, that I'll be leaving her before long as I turn my fate around. She knows. We're quits.

The first thing she does is to pick up the phone and fill her friends' ears with gossip picked up the previous day. And your daughter? My son-in-law? My jewels? My pennies? A cackling of society hens with lukewarm excesses. Women hardened by money and characterless destinies. Frustration, vanity and pretension succeed one another in a bland, horrified, hopeless saraband. There is something depressing about these overfull but lacking lives.

After a long list of kidnappings, deaths and money stolen from the state coffers, a well-known journalist announces on the radio in a trembling voice that this island is home to an empire of evil. Unable to control herself, Madame Herbruch calls up two of her friends to comment on this news and consider departing for

Miami. All her customers, all her friends want to flee to Miami. It has always been a good time to flee from this country, but who could really do it? I imagine Miami as a new Garden of Eden, the refuge for all those who have escaped an earthquake, leaving behind them the dead and the wounded.

When she wants me to rally to her cause I give her my wholehearted agreement. Perhaps a little too enthusiastically – she understands from my expression that I do not share her enthusiasm. That I am one of the dead and the wounded she would not hesitate to abandon. She understands that I am lying to her. My expressions have always betrayed me. From the start I have always reacted instinctively to things and to people. As I grew I did it as a matter of defiance. And then, deep inside, I came to know that the elation and pleasure of the conquerors will end up suffering a great fall as a result of always wanting more. That by always wanting more they have now reached a point of despair that they don't even realise themselves, a point of deep-down certainty that the kindness and gentleness of the defeated could at any moment turn and drive them, the conquerors, into a place of fear. The conquerors know this, and so do the defeated. And because of it we, both defeated and conquerors, are today equal in our despair.

I don't know what conclusion my boss draws as she looks at me, but she does not say a word. From the depths of her gilded cavern she seems to be calling for help. Her face is twisted into a grimace that she has invented on the spot, intended for me alone. Recovering possession of herself, Madame Herbruch applies her fuchsia-coloured lipstick, powders her face and leaves, hardly bothering to say goodbye to me. I savour the temporary pleasure of this brief victory. For the moment it's all I have. And I'm happy with it.

TWENTY-ONE

In the tap-tap we are pressed together thigh against thigh, flank against flank, forced despite ourselves into a malodorous, grudging embrace. People are talking nineteen to the dozen and this wild jaunt is soon transformed into a theatrical performance. They all have something to say about their prowess, their exploits, their cunning and that male or female wisdom that allows them to see further than ordinary mortals. How could anyone see that far and not have made their escape from this galley? I ask you. But none of us, myself included, has the courage to ask these comedians to be quiet, to call to mind the only subject that would make us come out with our truths like a decayed tooth pulled once and for all. Because another conversation, a silent one, is weaving its way among us – in the shadow of our guts, the redness of our blood, the obscurity of our bones.

We know full well what is being hatched by our flesh torn by suffering, our black-nailed hands, our gashed heels, our threadbare clothes, our gap-toothed gums, the sweat that sticks to our skin. We know. And so we continue the conversation elsewhere, in the intimacy of kerosene lamps whose glow makes our faces seem as if devoured by rats. When our shadows dance against the rough walls of our houses we will raise the subject of the secret evil that has been advancing over two centuries. Later, later, once we are within our own walls.

The time for stifled voices is back. *Le temps de se parler par signes.* The time of unbearable absences. Here we are, all three of us, caught between fear and anger. Hope and despair. We do not yet know that our first hardships are still within an inch of our happiness. We do not yet know that the waiting could kill with stealth.

When a man with a thick bull's neck and a T-shirt with the image of the leader of the Démunis gets into the tap-tap and sits down, the lively conversation seems to be inflamed. The more it becomes inflamed, the more it loses all savour, while the other, the silent one, comes to life, flares up in our chests. We want to jump onto the neck of this man, to shout out our exhaustion and to tear off his T-shirt. I take a deep breath and close my eyes. But we are weak. Some more weak than others. We are indignant, we stifle our shouts. But we are weak.

The events of the previous day, those of the morning, have shaken up our hearts a little more. Fearing as we pass the young, cruel faces of these children who already have death at their fingertips, we hurry on despite ourselves. Death has already filled their eyes so many times that they destroy to assure themselves of their own existence. Destroy or themselves be destroyed. Frighten or be frightened. Fear has become the most subtle vigilance, an implacable sovereign. The radios do not tell of it all. It is impossible for them to tell of everything. Death travels more quickly than the news, bulletins and the latest reports.

Who will ever know that a sixteen-year-old, graced with one of those nicknames from Hell, A-bullet-to-the-head, one day begged Aunt Sylvanie for help? Who will ever know? His emotion was such that his lips were trembling and words were pouring from his mouth as if he wanted to clear them out, like a poison that was scorching his tongue and his insides. When Aunt Sylvanie asked him what he wanted from her, he replied that he wanted to be able to sleep in peace. He could no longer shut his eyes at night, since he had severed with a

machete the hands and legs of a youth in his neighbourhood who was trying to run away, before pushing him,
alive, into the flames of his burning house. Since he had
planted his member inside Marie-Laure, the daughter of
the head of the only school there. Marie-Laure started
out fighting like a young bird caught in a trap. She cried
out, her head knocking against a wall at every thrust of
the hips, then finally passed out when the third of the
gang members, sated, gave a final grunt and left her for
dead. Throughout this account, A-bullet-to-the-head
was talking jerkily, gasping for breath. His chest was
moving up and down as if he were winded, and he
begged Aunt Sylvanie to surround him with the protection of the Invisibles because from that moment he was
afraid – despite the interventions of a healer, a boko who
had demanded a frizzle chicken, three grey tortoises and
a black candle. Despite the blessed image he carried in
his right trouser pocket, the one in his left and the one in
his shirt pocket – one to ensure that he does not miss his
victims, another to make sure he gets paid on his return
and the third to keep him from ever getting caught. At
first he had been well stoked up, by the dope, the jour-
nalists of the Prophet President's radio and the authorities who were bigger than him.

'In the end the dope possesses you. Your guardian
angel abandons you, leaving you alone on the vast plain
of life, driven away.' He paused for a moment, heaving a
great sigh before continuing, gazing into the distance, his
hands calmly resting on his thighs. 'You can't resist the
oppressive voices of the radios, nor the furious voices of
the authorities. It's impossible to resist lectures like
that!!!'

Her lips pressed together tightly, face impassive
beneath her scarf, Aunt Sylvanie did not try to interrupt
him once.

'At first you're more afraid of blood than of those they

send you to kill,' he said. 'Then you're even more afraid of the anger of the authorities than of the blood and then after that you're no longer afraid of anything at all... Until the day when death catches up with a few like me and takes away our sleep.'

Cars overtake us at speed, some of them with sirens blaring, guns poking from their windows. We all, the driver included, take up positions that ensure we do not meet the eyes of the passengers in these vehicles that paint a new face on an old disaster with which we are all too familiar. One day, someone in this city must have given a signal for disorder and ever since then there has been no respite. No safety catch. The order of time, of space has not returned since. And today this city continues its inexorable progress into horror.

Our tap-tap is stopped by four youths in rags who are soon joined by quite a horde swarming around the vehicle. Without a moment's hesitation they attach themselves to the bonnet and the doors, dancing and yelling out their excitement. Their faces covered with bruises, their feet and calves with cuts. They twist, remove and smash everything in their reach, man-made objects, public or private property, bodies and souls. And this afternoon they are armed to the teeth.

Two of them take aim at us, each with a gun he can hardly hold in his hands. They are barely twelve, thirteen, fourteen years of age. Young adults who have only just arrived on the scene are carrying automatic weapons and cartridge belts on their thin shoulders. They have scarves wound around their heads and wear shades, no doubt stolen, that swallow up their faces, with second-hand jackets and T-shirts that are too big for their frail bodies: Nike, Puma, Adidas. The man with the bull's neck wearing the T-shirt with the image of the leader of the Démunis exchanges a sign of recognition with them. They twist their hands and wrists and give out a resounding 'Yo', a kind of war cry of complicity. My vision becomes blurred. My ears are ringing. I am overcome by dizziness. The youths have surrounded the tap-tap and are threatening us with their guns while the younger kids calmly strip us of everything that comes to their hands. I hold out my purse and my earrings. I would have held out anything. And then things happen quickly, very quickly.

The driver takes off at speed, happy to be alive. As we are. The silence that follows is filled with shame and anger. Other tap-taps surge into the alleyways in an icy panic. All that can be heard is the sound of engines. The exhaust gas burns our eyes. I crouch down into my seat until I can no longer be seen from the street. Next to me on my right there is an elderly man whose lips are still trembling, mumbling out disjointed words in a low voice, while to my left are two building workers, who will no doubt have handed over their tools and their day's pay, and behind me a young university student who has clearly not yet read the book that will give him the key to what he has just experienced, an explanation to show him the way. I can't help thinking of a song I heard the other day:

I have no work, I don't need it.
I was born to steal your money.
I was born to kill you.

Nothing will ever be the same again. Nothing. No-one will believe any more in the miracles of the rains or the blossoming of the trees. No-one. We are heading towards the night, in the silence of stone, the muteness of tombs.

Eyes half-closed, I want to be silent to swallow my shame. Any further and we would all have soiled our underwear. Myself included. And we would have sat in our filth without flinching. We have lost all self-respect.

But you can get used to anything, even losing your self-respect.

I am becoming a woman who doubts. This evening, I will kneel on the ground at the foot of my bed and I will humbly ask God to forgive my lack of faith in the work of the men of this place, as His ways are so mysterious. Eyes closed, head nodding, I silently murmur a hymn and cannot stop myself from asking God to help me, humble creature that I am, never to doubt.

TWENTY-TWO

Whatever catastrophes the radios foretell, I do my best to distance myself from their predictions, to deny their effect on my life. Once Madame Herbruch has left I choose a station that plays nothing but music to forget by, and lose myself in a zouk to ward off all these prophecies. And I think long and hard about my next chance to go dancing with Lolo. The next chance to find myself face to face with Luckson like on that first evening when, without telling me he desired me, without him knowing how much I wanted him, we finally tasted each other's lips, savoured one another's skin.

It was at the Groove Night Club, a crowded disco between a smelly ravine and a makeshift school. Lolo had persuaded me without much difficulty to go with her that evening. Fignolé's band, who were starting to make a name for themselves, were playing there for the first time. A few young people were jostling one another by the entrance. I remember how happy I was to see my younger brother's budding success. And for a few months now there had been Ismona, dawn and dusk, rain and shine. I rushed to his side to congratulate and encourage him. And although he hugged me with incredible tenderness, I felt he was as absent as ever. Fignolé was visibly elsewhere. He had crossed the borders of the world beyond which ghosts come to find us. He had left us to float on his cloud. But that night the cloud was on fire. Fignolé's eyes were glowing like a city in flames, and Fignolé was not a man to recoil from a fire he had lit himself. No way! There's nothing for it, Fignolé's hooked, I told myself. And to be hooked is to be a touch below the condition of being mortal. It is to be chased from Paradise a second time. Yet Fignolé has created a quarantine, I don't know by what miracle, and succeeded in preserving a clear spirit, one of sanity amidst the confusion, the abandonment, the great tropical disorder. I feel it at the same time as I am gripped by the certainty that life will crush him. Soon. Very soon. Because life kills pure hearts first of all. This certainty made itself felt so strongly that I was submerged in that strange anxiety that sometimes catches drunkards unawares and settles right in the middle of their happiness.

I had never seen Fignolé with such an expression, never. And I was scared. I went hot, cold, then hot again. There was no longer a drop of blood in my veins, nothing but hot, liquid fear. This fear could have devoured me from the inside if I had not suddenly shaken it off and sent it away. I devoured it first. I inoculated myself with all the arrogance of my youth. One by one, I treated the bites of anxiety. I slowly filed down the sharp claws of fear. I slowly breathed in an incredible force to hold me steady. To hold me on my feet, on my high heels. And I danced through the night, danced to exhaustion.

Lolo had arranged with Paulo to get us one of the tables right next to the band. We had hardly sat down there where the first males came round on their inevitable prowl. With the intention, who knows, of stealing from Lolo and me a bit of our flesh in a night that looked set to be long and turbulent. That's how men are. And Jean-Baptiste was one of those who is not content simply to prowl. He followed my every step. He was hunting me down. Whatever I did I was observed, spied on, tracked. Lolo immediately suggested I had a drink.

'I'm just not getting you tonight. You need a drink,

otherwise you'll never be on the same plane as us.'

The drink fizzed in my throat and made me cough slightly, reawakening the fleeting shadow I'd felt. Then cheerfulness took hold little by little. I could once again raise my eyes and face all those stares. Especially that of Luckson. Luckson, who was carried along by the night. Standing in silence, exuding strength. I was enraptured by his presence. I sensed eyes on me, calling me. Eyes for which I was prepared to be damned on the spot.

The band played as the curtain was raised. We danced to the sounds of Fignolé's compositions and covers of Bob Marley, Shaba, Alpha Blondy. Fignolé played like never before, as if he were playing for the final time in his life. As if it were his last will and testament. And I was once again gripped by the beauty and gentleness of his latest composition. Music and lyrics in which the spirit can roam, elated and wondering. A gathering-place for all the ancient forces, all the age-old powers. Fignolé wanted them to come and take him over, move through him, submerge him and drag us all in his wake. I felt the little grey stone inside me slowly melt into indulgence and elation. We danced in an extraordinary joy and excitement. The music moved me, carried me away, made me reel, while the boys tried to grab me by the waist each time I got close, closer. We were a little crowd come together there who, for the space of an evening, refused to think of the hardships of the moment, and closed the doors on the shadows outside.

After the band's set a DJ excelled himself and literally set the room on fire with the music of Janesta.

And while I danced and spun, surrounded by bodies, Fignolé watched me from behind his cloud of smoke and smiled at Ismona. Luckson came up to me and never took his eyes off me. It was strange to be able to look at him so close up and to be looked at by him. Luckson didn't dance. He didn't need to. Luckson knew that this young woman passing from hand to hand was a burning torch. Luckson knew I was already dazzled. Already enraptured by him. He knew. But I did not smile at him. I did not speak to him. I could be lost at the slightest smile, or at the slightest word. And I don't want to be lost.

Ismona joined me and we laughed our hearts out between these two men.

TWENTY-THREE

Port-au-Prince has planted poisoned seeds in me and the deadly tree will not stop growing, growing. Port-au-Prince has slipped away from us like water running through our fingers. Disorder has gnawed away at every inch of this land and it is now a disorder of the soul. We cannot get better. Perhaps we don't want to? In the outlying districts a boy of twelve is an old man: he has already dispatched two or three human beings over the precipice into eternity and has brains scorched by the ether. He has seen too much, heard too much, done too much. A girl of thirteen is a worldly woman with two or three lovers to her credit and has already helped boys to fill the void of death. And if hardship comes knocking at your door one day, don't even think of complaining. Those appointed to the defence of victims are experts in red tape and pull them apart to the bone. That will not stop me this afternoon – I, Angélique Méracin, daughter of Venante Méracin – from going to the police station to report the disappearance of my brother Fignolé. And if he does not return before nightfall, tomorrow I will register a complaint against persons unknown. It's a matter of principle. 'A complaint against persons unknown' is a formula I hear on the radio and from the lips of lawyers. I will at least have the satisfaction of keeping to a principle in a country full of 'maybes', of 'keep your head down', of 'ifs' and of 'you never know which way the wind will blow'.

In the darkness behind my closed eyelids I have not

been able to stop myself from thinking of Fignolé. Where are you, Fignolé? Please give us a sign.

Tell the bad girl and the prodigal son that they can come home if they hurry.

Disappointment in the Démunis made Fignolé bitter at first, then mad with rage. I suspect he also wanted to lose himself in love affairs I will not name, to court death. As he waits, he blinds himself with the dope he breathes in, which gives him wide, slack eyes. Detached from the circles of mortals, he falsely believes he can join the gods and forget us all. But there's nothing for it, Fignolé, the world will get you. It always gets us. But I promise you now that when the world gets you I will be by your side. I promise, I swear. And I will know how to take your hands in mine like when you were tiny and took your first steps. I will know how to warm you with words like Joyeuse. Yes, exactly like Joyeuse. By your side I will swell the ranks of the chosen. I will be one of yours... I'm rambling, I'm rambling... I know I'm rambling. A lump is forming in my throat. And my thoughts turn to that other youth whose eyes I have just closed on an eternal night. How can I forget him? How can I forget Fignolé, of whom we have heard nothing since yesterday evening? I don't know what he does with his evenings when he leaves, guitar under his arm. Or rather, I do know. Yes, I do know really. I suspect. I imagine. As if I were by his side, behind him, in his shadow. Like I'm beginning to inhabit the shadow of that sick man lying on a hospital bed.

Through the windows I see the sky bring down the colourful canvas of the sunset. And I am held by these fixed moments in a strange, celestial stupor. These minutes, summoned only to sweep so quickly into the great void of the other side. I have nothing left but words of survival that break against my teeth, and this day that is disrobing itself with the movements of a damaged tree.

As I approach the house I have neither name nor face. The afternoon has smashed inside me into thousands of glass fragments. Fragments glowing with colour – mauve, pink and yellow – that spin, whirl and all but suffocate me.

A flock of birds streaks the sky.

I get down from the tap-tap and I see in the distance the afternoon bleeding into the blue horizon.

TWENTY-FOUR

It must have been midnight when a young man, standing in the entrance to the Groove Night Club, made a sign to Jean-Baptiste. I couldn't make out his silhouette too well in the half-light, and I don't know why I followed Jean-Baptiste. Concealed in a corner by the door, I caught the first few words of one of those stories that leave no room for doubt – men going off to kill or be killed. Jean-Baptiste was leaning against a tree by the main entrance and I could see from the fire in his eyes that he felt a brutal delight in anticipation of this chase. Jean-Baptiste doesn't have a thought in his head, I said to myself at the time, he has nothing but urges. All it took was for a few acquaintances to chance by one day with a fistful of dollars, some girls and a set of wheels for him to return to the wretched gang. It would be no mistake to think of him simply in terms of a body – one made for pleasure, clothes and violence. And that evening I was as certain of the latter as of two and two making four. Intrigued and disturbed, I went back to the noise of the party.

At the other end of the hall, Luckson, sitting at our table, did not take his eyes off me. And I could no longer quieten my rising desire for him. A harsh, painful desire. For the first time I felt pain as I approached a man. For the first time I was afraid as I approached a man. And I wanted to keep hold of this pain and this fear which made me feel good like I never had with anyone before him. I remember placing my hand on the table as I stood there facing up to his stare. He lit a cigarette and ordered a beer. He watched me from behind the wreaths of smoke that he concentrated on blowing out from time to time with rounded lips. His stubbornness enchanted me. And I matched it with a stubbornness of my own coursing through my veins. At that precise moment in the night we were like two deranged wrestlers, each refusing to yield an inch of ground to the other. We fought with an intensity equal to our desire for one another. We were on the verge of reeling from this test of strength. And I repeated to myself over and over: 'I can wait, however much I want you, Luckson.'

After a few minutes of this game, Luckson came up to me and I suddenly realised my outer defences were badly guarded. But instead of patrolling my boundaries I attacked my opponent full on. I smiled at him. Having tested it out on others I had overestimated the effect of my weapon. Luckson placed an authoritative hand on my hip and gently pulled me against him. He led me outside. I recognised the old banger belonging to the neighbour who had taken me home after our first meeting. The car moved through dark streets, in the voluptuous obscurity of the night. Men, women and houses streamed by the windows. The old car spluttered out black, noxious smoke and made a deafening noise. The infrequent passers-by turned to watch us pass. I wished these hazy images would never end. I had entered another game, intense, extravagant. Lulled by the motion of the car, I was departing on a long voyage. The others, all the others were left behind, tied to the dock. In my detachment, the world could no longer touch me. I had loosed my moorings. I was drifting gently.

Luckson parked the car outside the same house at the end of the narrow alleyway. And just like the first time he simply told me in his husky, almost savage voice:

'Come on.'

TWENTY-FIVE

The gallery is east-facing and always in the shade in the afternoons. On my return I sit myself down in the corner I have arranged for myself just to the right, where a section of wall hides me from the curiosity of passers-by. I hear Gabriel, as if from behind a curtain of mist, kicking a ball with a few of the neighbourhood kids, shouting at the tops of their voices. I recall those evenings when we would turn our backs on the commotion of the adults' world and Mother would lead us in her deep, cavernous voice into the phosphorescent blue world of dreams, evoking all the fears, the scandals and the marvels rooted deep inside us, stories of ogres and blood, of the blue-tinted, diaphanous marvels of our origins. Beneath the watchful eye of the moon in the back yard, or the golden lights that danced beneath the gallery, we would fall asleep like happy young savages immersed in the feats of heroes, vivid images of joy, the secrets of plants, the voyages of the galipotes, the beauty of flying fish and phosphorescent shells. I remember a certain evening. We were sitting beneath a December sky, the Tropics' most beautiful. And we were gazing, fascinated, at the thousands of stars. We also listened to the mongrel dogs of the streets howling out their dread of death, the voices of men clouded by alcohol, the cries and laughs of women. We were immersed in all that, Joyeuse, Fignolé and I: separations, pain, deprivation, injustice and death. And yet the world still smelt of innocence. The time had not yet come when the imminence of disaster caused cracks to appear in Fignolé's joyful nature.

Faced with the irremediable and the infernal, the three of us reacted in different ways: Fignolé with absolute bravado, stubbornly creating a distance from the seductions that sought to offer forgetfulness of the world's cruelties. Joyeuse with indirect confrontation. And I in submission to the world as God had created it.

Today, I have broken with my usual routine and have not changed out of my uniform or shoes because I have to go to the police station to find out what has become of Fignolé. I have contented myself with sitting down to get my bearings. And this afternoon I really need to do that. To touch base with my centre of gravity. Define my destination. Follow my compass. Rediscover my balance and set my course. Life has been so difficult for some time. On this island. In this district. So difficult between the walls of this house.

I feel as if I am in free fall, drawn by a strong, invisible force like that which controls the movement of the planets, the rotation and revolution of the Earth. And I feel far too insignificant to set up any resistance to it. After all, these events are a response to the divine destiny written in the movements of the stars. But what about me in the middle of all that?

> *See, the name of the Lord comes from afar*
> *With burning anger and dense clouds of smoke*
> *He places in the jaws of the people a bit that leads them*
> *astray.*

For the first time I feel that these words of the Apocalypse contain more truth than usual. That the end has not yet come, but that all these events herald it. The moment when the shadows no longer allow the day through. When the angel with gigantic wings will blow on that silver trumpet and proclaim in a loud voice that time is no more.

A painful omen has silently taken its place in my heart. I suddenly feel a desire to fall into a sleep deeper than the deepest well. More silent than the surface of Lake Azuei. More regular than the roundness of an orange.

I do not hear Mother arrive. She places a hand on my shoulder and sits by my side. She launches straight into reminding me that I should go to the police station to report Fignolé missing. There is a moment of silence. The silence that waits for words to emerge from our dreams, these words that nightfall will bring. We cling obstinately to our reluctance to speak of this thing, as if each wants to protect the other from a burden too heavy to bear. And yet this thing has the capacity to bring us together like never before in the love of a single man.

Mother is a loving Mother. She loves us today more than yesterday and tomorrow better than today. She loves us to distraction because in this city she knows that she could lose us at any moment.

'Today, when you set foot outside this house you are like a Borlette number; you don't know if you will return. Today everyone walks with their coffin under their arm because death is no longer confined to the shadows beneath the earth. With its heart on its sleeve, in full day-light, it moves up and down the streets of this city and when the time comes for you to recover yourself on meeting it, you will be as stiff as a corpse.'

I gather all my strength to place one foot in front of the other and make my way to the police station, leaving Mother to her prayers. She will call Madame Jacques and the murmuring of their litanies will mount to the sky like the humming of bees. They will pray, turning the rosary beads over and over until their throats are dry and their fingers blistered.

The presence of Willio as I enter the police station is reassuring. Willio introduces me to his colleagues. Despite everything, the Commissioner on duty thinks nothing of making me wait for over an hour. It's a crazy thing about this country that you have to wait for authorities who are always busy or rushed and who send you away until tomorrow 'if God wills it'. I assiduously watch this servant of the State charged with guaranteeing us the protection of the Republic. He weighs me up at first glance, concluding that it will be difficult to get anything from me by way of a backhander. He tries giving me a knowing look. He attempts the energy and charm he uses on those young madams who pace up and down, up and down, along the corridors of public administrations. I remain aloof and I don't think that pleases him. He will try to extract from me a sum of money we don't have, but for which we would be ready to get into a decade's worth of debt if we had to.

When my turn comes I sit across from him and try not to repeat to myself the conclusion I have gained from watching him: you clearly have a past that is not squeaky clean, and a similar present. And there is no chance of this state of affairs changing in future.

'I have come to report the disappearance of my brother Fignolé Hermantin, age twenty-one.'

He tells me to sit without even raising his eyes. And from the way he replies 'Wait a moment' I know in advance that I will lose this round. A few moments later, at a sign from him, I continue by stating Fignolé's age and occupation, describing a few of his physical characteristics, his size and his hair with its heavy dreadlocks. This last trait clearly does not please him, as his mouth tightens with displeasure. I remain impassive.

The Commissioner listens to me distractedly then favours me with a 'Call later' and then a 'Come back tomorrow'. I would perhaps have more of a chance if he said to me: 'My price is so much. How much are you prepared to pay?' But he doesn't and I don't let him. I don't have the means, and in that case he would ask me to pay with the only asset I have in his eyes. I wouldn't do that, either.

His voice dies away at the same time as anger and despair stifle me. I leave the police station at the same moment as Jean-Baptiste gets in there, giving a very friendly greeting to the commissioner and his men who seem delighted to see him. Surprised by my presence, he tries to reassure me, taking my hands and telling me that he will set things rolling through contacts with people in high places.

'Yes of course, Jean-Baptiste, of course…'

And for the first time I see Jean-Baptiste as he really is. A dancer of the compas, the laloz, the gayé pay and the salsa. Pretentious, sensual and, today, dangerous.

Willio is waiting for me at the entrance to the station and clearly wants to tell me something. He comes up to me and simply whispers in my ear:

'Never set foot in this place again, Miss Angélique. Never again.'

TWENTY-SIX

As he opened the door his hand brushed against mine, leaving a bite-like tingle on my skin. Luckson then whispered a few inconsequential words in my ear, words that melted into one another: 'your lips, you, want'. A river burst its banks inside me and the desire for this man burst through my veins in thousands of tiny bubbles. I said 'My love' to him without thinking, as if I were singing. In a low murmur. I undid my blouse myself. In my haste I missed a button. My boldness surprised him at first and then pleased him, so much that his face creased up in a grin of admiration and pleasure.

Luckson undressed me like someone dying of thirst peels an orange. Pressing his lips against my breasts, my stomach, slipping his hands towards that dark triangle between my thighs. My body slowly came to life beneath his fingers and his mouth. His touch left feverish traces on my aroused skin. I offered my stomach to his lips, my breast to his brow. His incipient beard tickled me and I let out a surprised laugh. I have never laughed with any of those other men whose fervour has flattered me, repulsed me or left me cold. Luckson's laugh is a favour. I don't know if I should seize it. I don't know… I float my face against his skin. And the Luckson holds me, firmly but gently. Firmly but very gently between his hips. Until the moment of that exquisite suffering that grips me and slowly turns me inside out.

Luckson is a man of will and a man of love, and I like that.

These thoughts skimmed over me, full like the geography of the clouds. I didn't want to hold on to any of them, especially not those which, in the blink of an eye, tried to trap me in a strange melancholy or that hint of happiness that sometimes follows our embraces. I very soon shook from myself both the melancholy and all temptation of happiness. Like the other girls of the inner-city suburbs I first learned the sensual pleasures of the flesh at a very early age. They have never been able to take away from me, soul that I am scoured from birth by deprivation, an inner mistrust of the happiness of books and the melancholy of the cinema.

After a moment I detached myself from Luckson's embrace. I looked at him, fascinated. I went to the bathroom and reapplied my lipstick. My lips were full as if I had just woken from a long sleep. My forehead was glowing. And I wanted to make my eyes lie. They were shining too brightly not to belong to a woman who has just been made love to. Who has just made love herself. My eyes were shining too brightly not to give me away. I looked at myself one last time and told myself in the mirror: 'My heart, you especially, don't get carried away, don't get carried away...'

But since then, despite myself, a force has grown against which I am helpless. A thought has taken root deep inside me, around an image, always the same one, the image of Luckson. Everyone around me may walk, breathe, smile, but I no longer see them walking, no longer hear them breathing, I am blind to their smiles. Whatever they do I no longer sense them approaching, seeking me out in their arrogance and hunger. No-one can cure me of Luckson. The earthquake has already happened.

I closed the doors of the shop earlier, at four o'clock precisely. I should call to see Uncle Antoine to warn him of

Fignolé's absence. I feel my strength leaving me. But I don't want to give in. I mustn't give in. I will go and see Luckson. Luckson's skin will make me forget. Luckson's slim thighs will make me forget. His bold hands. Luckson is missing me. He is waiting for me somewhere in this city…

Black-skinned and from a poor background, Uncle Antoine used this despised colour and low origins as an incontestable argument for robbing the State and committing one wrong deed after another. Every day, without respite and without a word, Aunt Léonide would keep Uncle Antoine from stumbling. After years of this thankless battle, Léonide Nériscat had become a sly, tough, falsely friendly person. Looking more closely, the task of Uncle Antoine and Aunt Léonide was harsh and allowed them no respite. So harsh that it had caused the hair of Antoine Nériscat to go white prematurely and had slowly eaten away at the eyes of his wife, leaving them surrounded by two deep, pallid hollows.

My conversation with Uncle Antoine is brief. I'm always nervous of talking to this uncle who would receive us, the poor, between the backyard and the kitchen. The wealth of Antoine Nériscat was always a subject of wonder for those of us whom poverty sought to entrap. Antoine Nériscat thought deep down that all those who were poor were only like that because they were unable to manage the range of tricks and schemes that were actually within reach. Or because they had got bogged down in those useless, endless considerations, justice and injustice, the master and the slave, as if they imagined that these things could have any weight in the reality of the world.

I tell him in a few words about our anxiety. We call Madame Jacques immediately. We are told that Paulo returned from Martissant more silent than he was when he left. We try our luck with the mysterious phone number and we get a police officer. Uncle Antoine knows that he has to make up a pretext on the spot. I can feel the ceiling sinking down until it crushes me. My heart will no longer stay in my chest. Uncle Antoine hangs up, frowning. Uncle Antoine doesn't like what has just happened. He must be scared. But in his eyes I can also see a great anger. And so Uncle Antoine, not knowing which to choose, his fear or his anger, finally launches into a diatribe against Fignolé's morals, his idleness, his foolishness and goodness knows what else. I sense that Uncle Antoine is on the verge of passing out. He is drooling and his lips are trembling. I tell him I have not come to see him this afternoon to talk about Fignolé but to find him. He shows me the door and leaves me with a remark, like throwing a bone to a dog: 'I'll have a word with my political contacts and keep you informed. Give my love to your mother and hurry home.'

Far from being solved, the mystery of my brother Fignolé is growing deeper.

TWENTY-SEVEN

After Gabriel was born, when I understood that the man with his shirt open to his navel and the gold tooth was not coming back, I filled a basin several times a day and washed and scrubbed myself. Again and again. Standing in front of the mirror I would scrutinise my body that had only just left behind the awkward lines of childhood, feeling each area of flesh, sniffing at my arms, my armpits, my thighs, my ankles. I was amazed not to find a single visible mark of the disgrace that was gnawing away at me, that I could feel etched into me with the cutting edge of a knife. There was no trace of pleasure left. I had left it dormant beneath my shame. The scent of a man, the sweat he had left on my chest, the semen mixed with blood, all these animal secretions impregnated my skin, contaminating me to the marrow. Inside me, rot was spreading, decaying.

This evening I scrub my body to rid it of death, to wash away the blood, to forget the shame. I want to clear a space for another day bathed in light by the water's edge. My body has stayed young despite an old, heavy weariness. Standing in front of the mirror I look at my face once again as if I had lost the memory of it for a long time. As if I were a kind of mould into which a history that was not mine had been poured. As if I were seeing this body for the first time. Yet I have existed for twenty-seven years. Twenty-seven years.

A woman's solitude makes her unsociable. Too unsociable. I need a man around whom my life would take on other colours. Not a man who would set my life on fire but a man who would come to me clothed in sun and rain. A rainbow man. A man for whom I would beat the rage out of my heart. A woman myself, I could face up to all other women for that man. I have measured my strength and I know it well.

Time passes and I can't bear to feel it passing, to feel at my back the seconds of an implacable clock ticking away. It sometimes makes me want to close my eyes, to curl up and die pitifully the death of an abandoned animal. My past is made up of days and events that don't seem to belong to me, that I didn't choose.

What stranger is already on his way, will come to reawaken in me the taste for minutes, the thirst for hours and the impatience for days...? A gesture would be enough. A single gesture... All he would have to do would be to look at me, tear down the walls. A man whom I would accept like an offering. Who would eat my meals and nibble my skin. Who would leave every morning to go conquer the world and at night would return to bury his man's fears in me. Whose weakness I would accept deep inside, as I would his strength. And already I feel this desire to shout out to him: Are you ever afraid? Do you like making love? Who are the women in your life? If you have any children, what are they called? Will you dream of me? Of my voice? My eyes? My breasts bent over you?

I think of my stranger. And immediately afterwards I think that I am a woman. That I am alive as a woman, not as anything else. That I have a body which can still be of use. That I carry inside me, coiled between my hips, that sole rampart against the sky, the most beautiful riposte to death. And I smile and even feel inclined to burst out laughing. A laugh that would rise up from the small of my back to my lips.

TWENTY-EIGHT

There is torment in this city. There is also intoxication. And there is this man who came into the world to get me lost. I hate the fact that I've let my guard down. I hate myself for being held under the sway of Luckson. I hate myself for foundering. For falling down to earth, to this mattress laid out on the ground.

Luckson has never told me that he likes me or that he is attached to me. Luckson's silence is more profound than the silence of other men. And so the memory of our movements suffices; that of our skin, too. There is the strength of my spirit, the lightness of my body. My spirit does not want to bend. My body seeks his. Desire makes my knees tremble. I am excited by my moments of wonder at Luckson. This man awakes in me the crazy idea of letting myself go.

Luckson is waiting for me. He opens the door and takes me by the hand, authoritatively. Forcing me to follow. I look at him with the full force of my gaze. When he sees me watching him so closely, his face opens up as if he would split in two. I look at him even more attentively. And I feel as if I will sink into that face. Taken by surprise, Luckson reaches out a hand to caress me on the cheek. And when he slides his thumb between my lips, I seize it between my teeth in a moment of sweet confusion.

I can't stop looking at that hand which pulled me out of the crowd. The wound he received that day has left a scar. I examine it like something I have never seen before, never come close to. I am held by fascination for that hand, by its gentleness.

I stretch out against Luckson. I close my eyes. Luckson asks me, placing his finger between my breasts:

'Tell me, how do you feel deep down inside, in the place where you keep your secrets?'

I say: 'Be quiet.'

He insists.

I repeat: 'Be quiet or I'm going.'

How can I tell him that I'm not wise? That my back is so fragile, so fragile…? That I'm burning up, destroying myself? That for all those who seek me out I agree to nothing but what they ask for, an outward appearance, a pretence – certainly not to this shadow that is calling inside me, this burial? That I have already gone beyond my blackness, well beyond? That this is the first time I have loved without caution? That I would lie at his feet? That I would want him to give me sleepless nights, days full of adventure, nights of ocean voyages and the exploration of deep forests. Days of wide-open spaces. Days in the belly of the sun. Instead of all this I murmur to him again,

'Be quiet, be quiet.'

And Luckson gets angry. He catches me by the shoulders and forces me to sit. He has lost that habitual calm that I have always taken for the aloofness of a young god. In his anger he is once again mortal, vulnerable. His face expresses his anger at the same time as an intense curiosity. I do not unclench my teeth. I dare not speak those bare words, defences down and without the night to mask them. It's too soon, too much. Luckson reprimands me with a gentleness of which he himself is unaware. Just as he is unaware how far that gentleness has brought me.

We do not exchange another word. Silence invades our story. In this silence I know that I will never forget

Luckson. Never. Just as I know that one day I will die. Just as I know that the moon will bathe the world in light, tonight, tomorrow night and all the other nights. Just as I know that Fignolé is missing and his absence is burning me up inside.

And then, Luckson, I reach out my hand to touch your face. Place my mouth on yours. I want to taste the salty breath of your life. You seek my lips to force out my secrets. My legs close tightly under the pressure of your hand. You do not sense my whole body recoiling. You don't see my desperate eyes open onto darkness. Even when, slowly, my body awakes beneath the gentle touch of your fingers, the force of your hips. Until that radiant disturbance floods into my belly. Until the vast, over-flowing, terrifying silence arrives, a silence I can hardly endure. As if the rushes of your body have reached me, to open me, flood into me and heal my soul. I do not want to be healed. I want to run away and cannot. I plant my nails into your skin to stop myself foundering.

We are so stupefied by gentleness, so overcome by pleasure that we look at one another like two strangers come from a distant land. The world has been broken apart by violence in our absence. You fall away. I bite down on the end of the mattress. And we allow the exhaustion of loving to take hold of us.

I leave there reeling, intoxicated with the question that at once delights me but makes me feel so bad: 'Luckson, why awaken a heart that nothing should be allowed to thrill? Why?'

Luckson has insisted on accompanying me because the streets are still not safe. The air outside is heavy. The sun has long since hidden its fingers in the crumpled sheets of clouds. And these clouds have invaded the world in a shadowy procession advancing on the impassive ground of earth, sea and sky. Luckson only breaks the silence to ask me to tell him if I hear the slightest news about Fignolé. He leaves me at the tap-tap station not far from the house. I do not turn to watch him go.

Night is already falling. I taste the night on my face and my hands, my arms and my legs. This taste that has taken a strange bite from my soul, leaving my senses in disarray. The dark night is full of murmurs, dreams, shouts and cries moving towards the heart of the dozing houses.

On the gallery I will sit between Angélique and Mother and I will say nothing for a long moment, or very little. And then, without us really thinking about it, a few words will arise from our dreams. In this silence and these words we will love one another deeply. We will also be all right. Almost despite ourselves. This is the only moment when Ti Louze will be given a brief respite, sitting on a step at the entrance to the house. She will finally bathe in the same humanity as we do. It is that moment of the day when we can listen to one another for hours. The moment of bald words, strong words. Without the trappings, without the props of the world. It is the hour when we will search for that word just out of reach or in the bloom of life. The words that come from these places are distant, sweet, shaken by laughter, ripped, burned, fragile, powerful, precious.

TWENTY-NINE

From the four corners of the city fires rise from rubbish piles and burn our eyes. Every evening at nightfall, pyromaniacs crucify the poverty of Port-au-Prince to preserve its silence. We proceed, pacified, half-blinded, in a deceptive fog. It is the moment when night descends on Mother's face. This unique face of one who will never leave, who will always stay near you, despite the storms over your life, despite the fire that lays it waste. Mother's face is a piece of soft earth, the ground on which we place our naked feet without fear of being hurt. Mother's desire to search through the night makes her a ship that cleaves through black water. She moves forward but goes nowhere. The silence inside her is as deep as that of the great belly of water beneath the sea. Has she lost the north? She is so afraid of capsizing. Yes, so afraid. From time to time the moon pours out its quicklime and, relieved, she scans the world in this white light. And once again she sets her course towards the wait for her son.

The night slowly tilts forward. I hear it falling with its music and its restraint. A night of Eden, a night from before the Fall. Huge emotions also fall with it. Mother speaks, perhaps, of her childhood that burned away so quickly, like a Bengal match. Whispers in ears in the dark, the sound of first steps towards the baskets gathered not far from the huts, the aroma of coffee made with a little water for Aunt Sylvanie and herself. Syrupy, black coffee as she still likes it, in the wispy colours of the old days. She walks in the footsteps of her mother, Sylvanie by her side. Three ebony candles sliding through the mother-of-pearl of the night. She does not refer to those who were broken in the sugar-cane fields of the Dominican Republic. Those buried in watery graves who never reached the other side. Those who stayed in the country of their childhood, what has become of them? She will not say that all the demands they ever made on earth have been in vain, the earth has not responded to their supplications.

Joyeuse arrives and joins us, lost in thought. I tell her in a few words about my visit to the police station. We babble among the shadows. We, women of too many words, swollen with so much silence. God, even our gestures are silent!

The words finally arrive. From afar. From far away. They come from the depths of solitude, and from even further away. They make us want to hold them in our hands so they will touch us with a closeness greater than that of an embrace.

The two kerosene lamps have not yet been lit. In truth, no-one has felt like lighting them. There are enough words, silence and dreaming to see ourselves from the inside. Passers-by can hardly make us out, but greet us: 'How are you, Ma Méracin?', 'Evening Miss Angélique', 'Any news, Joyeuse?' The world moves on at its own pace. Deep in contemplation, we do not see Paulo arrive, but we hear him bellowing like a beast. On hearing Paulo's cries, the three of us know that a great calamity is on its way towards us.

'They've killed Fignolé!' he yells three times in a row.

Ti Louze quickly lights the two lamps. The first shadows dance in their orange glow. We can make out Paulo's features clearly. He is unrecognisable. His pain seems to have been carved into his bones with the point of a knife. Vanel, the drummer in the band, is holding him up like an old man at the end of his strength and says between sobs he can hardly hold back: 'I was there.'

Mother doesn't say a word but her mouth emits an indescribable sound that must have originated in her belly, made its way up through her chest, stifling her as it reached her throat and spurting out through her mouth. Then nothing. The help of two men is needed to revive her and to wind a cloth around her waist to bed the pain down in a nest inside her, let it begin to run its course like a child carried in her womb. Madame Jacques ties a scarf around her hair.

Vanel collapses onto a rickety chair and cannot hold back the story.

'I was just about to help Madame Guérilus, Ismona's mother, to close the double doors at the entrance to her house when four men came and stood in front of us. Civil guards, they were, in short-sleeved, sweat-stained T-shirts, wearing caps and trainers. Two of them were brandishing machetes and the older two each had an automatic rifle. The most forward of them, the one who must have been their leader, stepped up. He raised his T-shirt to reveal a nine-millimetre handgun next to his naked belly.

"Close up, close up quickly," Madame Guérilus shouted. "Close up quickly!"

'We had no time and I had to leg it away down an adjoining passage to the house and warn Fignolé and Ismona. Fignolé had no chance to run. Alerted by the cries of Madame Guérilus, he told Ismona to take refuge on the roof. It was too late for him to go back into the house and the balance of strength was hardly in his favour. So he decided to cover our escape through the nearby alleyways. Grabbing a machete, he hit the first of the assailants who'd forced their way into the back yard. Fignolé then jumped over a wall and joined us. We came up against a dead end at the other side of the neighbourhood, so we decided to separate to give ourselves a better chance of escape. I saw him disappear into the night, with no idea that I'd never see him again. The assailants divided into two groups as well. The first followed hot on our tails while the second went into the house, like professionals who were used to this kind of operation. One of them stood by Madame Guérilus and ordered her to be quiet. Immediately. The ringleader even said "I won't tell you twice."'

I am gripped by a deep despondency. My legs are trembling, my head spinning. I don't hear the end of Vanel's account. But I understand that there is a name he is reluctant to say out loud.

'I saw... I saw...'

He is crying hot tears like a child but the syllables we are waiting for do not pass his lips.

'Tell us, who?'

He is obviously terrified, so we do not insist. We all pretend not to want to know more. Except Joyeuse. She stares at Vanel. Joyeuse is reaching the end of her tether. Joyeuse is always at the end of her tether. Vanel knows he will not escape Joyeuse, even this evening as he avoids her gaze and cries with his eyes lowered.

The death of Fignolé is no longer something that is likely to happen. It has happened. This evening my wait, my anxiety, has ended. I am surprised to be almost relieved by this idea. Even with a great hole in my chest, I am relieved. Even though he is alone in his mystery and I am here in this thick fog with which his death had surrounded me. We will no longer stop him dying. We have not been able to find the words to persuade him to live.

Neighbours drawn out of their houses by our cries are arriving in a procession and gathering around the gallery and the back yard. We fill the night with a heartrending clamour. Willio and Jean-Baptiste, detained in the police station, will learn the news during the night or tomorrow morning. The house is full to bursting. Lolo holds Joyeuse in her arms and rocks her gently. Other neighbours continue to arrive with mournful, heavy steps, crossing the face of the night to celebrate death, eternal and forever encircling the city, as if this city were in a different time, an age from before the world began. As if this place were an idea born from Genesis.

Mother is rocking her upper body backwards and forwards after screaming as if her guts were being drawn out of her. She has begun a strange chant that emerges from the base of her throat, her lips sealed. Our neighbours, come to contribute their sobs and cries, follow her in this commotion of sounds and strangled cries.

I have to change my clothes. Boss Dieuseul and Maître Fortuné do not want me to go alone to reclaim my brother's body from the authorities; they want to go with me. God alone knows what the beast is capable of! Joyeuse rakes through the bottoms of drawers to scrape up enough to buy a bottle of rum from Madame Jacques. Of course Madame Jacques refuses the money and offers the bottle, the giblets, the watercress and the plantains for the broth. Lolo wants to take charge of all the next day's meals. Joyeuse has also thought of the tisane of ginger and cinnamon that the women will sip until dawn. Boss Dieuseul has set up the domino table by the entrance to the house himself. Once they have reached the necessary state of intoxication, the men will reminisce about Fignolé's extravagances, his life in the face of death. In this sadness that eats us up inside. In the glow of the kerosene lamps which shed great shadows across our faces as if they have been half gnawed away by rats.

I move in a desert like Jesus and all my personal temptations merge into one: I want to cry out to God that I do not believe he exists. Instead of this I close my eyes and my mouth on my blasphemy. I hear myself saying in the voice of a stranger: 'My God, let Your will be done!'

THIRTY

It is Fignolé's eyes that I will remember. The eyes of childhood sunshine. Then the eyes of the night. Traced by shadows, deep as a cavern. Looking at him you could hardly hold yourself steady on the lip of that abyss. What did you burn in your joints, Fignolé? I sought in vain to find the sun to light up your eyes. To intoxicate your ghosts. To thwart all those disturbing snares that had been set for you. I want to move through the grass and the pebbles to raise your eyes. Fignolé, you are a will-o'-the-wisp who will always appear dancing in my dreams. Perhaps we have to be born twice to live a little, only for a little. The first time by tearing the flesh, the second time by wounding the heart. See me, alone, with this heart you have left me with. Nothing but love for you, my little dead brother.

You appeared out of the night, a stubborn child of an earth that knows how to close its eyes to its crimes, so as to shut out the tumultuous world that hurt your ears so. To no longer be aware of ancient resentments, yesterday's distress, the bayahondes of fear. Were you singing your last reggae composition as you watched death advance?

I imagine you tearing along, your head full of dreams, insisting on a future, your head bent forward like a young bull. Did you ask to be beaten till they drew blood, beaten to a pulp? What images played out behind your eyelids? What corner of the moon lit you up for the last time? I wish so much that I had been able to sit by your prone body, holding you tight in my arms. Placing my hand on the wound to your heart. Stitching it back together with my fingers. Your thirst my thirst. Feeling against my neck your laboured breathing, your dying breaths. And crying against you, my only one.

Ti Louze is sitting on a step at the entrance to the house. A little heap of hardship lost on that step. Tears come to her eyes. She misses Fignolé and knows that she no longer has a single hope between these walls. Gabriel, sitting by her side, cries in silence. I am worried about Angélique. She is trembling so hard that I believe her bones are rattling together inside her body. Mother has proved to be stronger than I would have believed her to be. And the neighbours have all rushed over to us. And we are together, united like never before as we share our meals of mourning, our drinks to make us forget the pain. And we tighten our belts to keep the vengeance inside. Vengeance that bends our backs, rocks our bodies, makes our eyes gleam; unbearable.

Mother let out a cry like something torn from the throat of a wolf. Like a call to murder. And it was the other mistress, Erzulie Dantor, she of the red eyes from too much crying, eyes bulging with anger, who made her shout out, beat her chest and tear her clothes. Once Erzulie was appeased, Mother allowed herself to be restrained like a captive beast. We tied a scarf around her head and encircled her waist with a big cloth, so that her grief would bed down and run its course like a child carried inside her. At first light tomorrow, Angélique will inform Father André. Our Father André. I will go and visit Aunt Sylvanie, to make sure she will help Mother prepare the Boule Zin ceremony. Mother herself will fill the gourds of water at the foot of the poto-mitan. Ridden by the spirits, she and Mother will stagger with rolling eyes, turn on their heels, collapse, dislocated like marionettes or silent as silk. Dressed all in white, ason in her hand, Mother will invite the divinities and the dead to leave their watery domain for words of foam, seaweed and salt.

The spirits and the dead speak to the living through the voice of those they possess, and Fignolé will confide his secret in us. And as she burns his guitar, his favourite T-shirt and his notebook at the feet of the Invisibles of the water, Mother will murmur to him: 'My son, you have given me everything, weariness, sweetness and desperation.'

Angélique, Mother and I have still not had time this evening to try and understand. To dig deeper. To stick the pieces of the story back together, the story of the end of our Fignolé. It will be between the three of us, alone, unwitnessed.

Fignolé, I miss you, I miss you like an amputated limb, like a stillborn child. Nothing can fill the space in which you moved, walked, sighed, spoke and cried out your pain to the world. Nothing can fill it. Nothing can replace your hand in my hair, your arm around my shoulders. Your voice that would tell me, 'Little sister, how I love you.'

I have collapsed by Mother's side but I have not closed my eyes on the night. The image of the revolver has risen up to haunt me from a deep, terrifying abyss. It is the only image that can drive out that of Fignolé. The only one. Sweat soaks my back as if I were affected by a raging fever. My nightshirt sticks to my skin. I doze for about ten minutes to give respite to my gritted teeth, my knotted throat, as if I had swallowed a fistful of shells. The skin of my legs is crawling. I rise from the bed, carefully so as not to wake Mother. But Mother is lying in the darkness, motionless, eyes wide open and staring at the ceiling. She seems like a statue beneath the sheets. I cover my shoulders with her old shawl and go out into the backyard.

My throat is tight with those fragments of shells that let nothing past. No sobs, no anger, no cries. An underlying strangeness, dry and cold. And deeper, in the hollow of my chest, my grey stone is becoming sharp, hard, brittle. In the night I had the feeling that it was hardening into a malicious presence. And this morning, for the first time, I taste hatred – a sublime feeling that warms my body like rum. I measure the depth of the evil and the infinite variety of its consequences: jubilation, euphoria and an indescribable sense of superiority that it gives when crowned with success.

The last act of my old life will be to send away Ti Louze without anyone knowing. I will put her in the care of the Sisters' orphanage, or somewhere else – far away from here, in any case. I owe it to Fignolé. The first act of my new life will be to leave Luckson after having waited for him so eagerly. I will do it without remorse. In the end, remorse is a misplaced vanity. Lolo is right.

I think of the other one. The traitor. The tight-fitting dress I will wear on that day. My high heels. The carmine red with which I will outline my lips, and the thing I will hide in my bag. I think of that traitor lying on my belly and breathing for the last time. I can already hear the shot. I can feel the lukewarm blood on my hands. I can see his eyes, disproportionately big, staring amazed at death.

I would have liked to be able to keep hold of all the first hours of my life. But it is too late. It has all already happened. Everything has already tipped towards death.

I hear Angélique waking. The night is cracking on all sides. Dawn is already here.

By way of an epilogue

In the shadow cast by the moon on the carcases of cars and the cracked walls of the houses, Fignolé runs, gasping for breath. His left eyelid is so swollen that it hides his eye and makes him unrecognisable. He cannot stop panting and his T-shirt is soaked in sweat. Blood running from a cut on his forehead, just above his good eye, blurs his vision. It is impossible for him to see where he is putting his feet. So from time to time he stumbles, picks himself up and continues, running harder. Two incisors in his upper jaw are loose and he can't stop himself from running the tip of his tongue again and again over the gaps in the gum. He remembers the blow dealt by his enemy. He thought for a moment that he would pass out. The confrontation had been vicious. His attacker, surprised, isolated, had not expected such determination from the young runaway. He provoked his attacker, taking him by surprise from behind. In the fight that followed he ended up grabbing his attacker's gun and shooting him down. Fignolé is not alone in this headlong flight. Ismona and Vanel are with him and have hidden behind an abandoned garage wall at the end of a tangle of muddy passageways in this neighbourhood at the end of the world.

Fignolé runs beneath the moon, broken in two, his hands holding his right side. Women, men, old folk and children, crowded behind windows and rickety doors, watch with bated breath. They have put out all lights and candles so as not to attract attention, to ensure that, later on, looking dry-eyed into the distance, they can reply to the men in uniform and their accomplices with submachine guns that they saw nothing, heard nothing. As for Fignolé, he keeps running, expecting nothing, nothing more... He reels, picks himself up and falls again, involuntary moans escaping from his chest. Winded, he wants to be able to stop so he can breathe properly. Gather his wits. But he thinks his ribs are fractured, so breathing deeply would cause him greater suffering. And the rest of his attackers are on his heels in their untiring pursuit. Holding his agonised ribs, he runs, endures, and keeps running...

The moon disappears behind opaque clouds. Dogs howl in the sudden darkness. Nothing is heard between the howls but the footsteps of the young runaway hurtling on his way, piercing the silence of the night. Lying low in their hovels, the people listen to the voice of death. A dreadful foreboding twists and turns the guts of the women, who wrap their arms around their bellies to stop themselves crying. Dreams have deserted the stupefied eyes of the children. The men rub their chins over and over, deep in thought, or clear their throats to put a bold face on things.

And when the moon reappears to bathe carcases, hovels and trash once again in its light, a passage between the shabby houses disgorges two men. They move towards him, the first in a police uniform and the second in a beige shirt and jeans. As they hear from their hiding place the voice of the second shouting out an order to the man in uniform, Vanel and Ismona are doubtful at first, but there is no denying the evidence of their ears: it really is Jean-Baptiste. Ismona sticks her head out just at the moment when Jean-Baptiste steps back to indicate the direction in which Fignolé has run. Vanel reacts quickly. Pulling Ismona closer to him, he places his right hand firmly on her lips and grips her neck with his left hand to stop her from breaking into sobs and betraying their presence. Ismona trembles as if ridden by one of our wild spirits. You know, one of those spirits who help people survive the cruelty of men.

From a distance Fignolé calls out the name of Jean-Baptiste, insulting him. The man in uniform beside Jean-Baptiste extends his arm, takes aim and squeezes the trigger. The bullet hits the young runaway in his left thigh. Screaming with pain, he still has the strength to drag his leg for a few metres. Standing now in the white light of the moon, the man shoots a second time. This time Fignolé, breathless, is hit full in the face. The explosion propels him beyond pain. His head seems to be thrust into the ether. He staggers backwards from the violence of the impact. His legs are raised from the ground and he collapses on his back, his eyes and skin torn away.

Stretched out on the ground, his face is nothing more than a pulp of blood mixed with a whitish substance oozing from his skull. The blood forms a viscous puddle around his left ear. Only the heavy dreadlocks and the curve of his beard indicate the place where his face used to be. A corpse set down between grass and stone, Fignolé is a giant dead bird.

Time has stopped, the length and breadth of this distanced earth, wild in its night. Way beyond the crazily shaking treetops. Beyond the phantasmagorical flight of the clouds. As far as the furthest boundaries of all the lands that Fignolé will never see. Never.

From their new hiding-place, in a narrow passage between two houses, they can no longer see their friend. The echo of the explosion rebounded from the rock into Vanel and Ismona's heads. Ismona bites into Vanel's hand and hangs onto him to stop herself falling. Wracked with sobs, Vanel rocks her gently in his arms. An excess of fear causes Vanel's bowels and bladder to release in a single action and he feels himself soiling his trousers. The shame of it! Petrified, distraught, he and Ismona can do nothing for now but listen to the shockwave that echoes, echoes endlessly, blending with the howling of the dogs in the night. The certainty of the death of their friend resonates in their chests and they feel inside the full force of the violence and their turn so close at hand, so close...

The white, milky light of the moon continues, impassive, to enshroud the world.

Glossary

Agoué: A water god in the vodou religion. A kind of Haitian Neptune who rules over the sea, its fauna and flora, and the boats which sail on it. Those who live from the sea's resources are also subject to him.

Ason: A small gourd filled with small bones, decorated with the colours of the loas and used by the officiant in vodou ceremonies.

Bayahondes: Thickets.

Blancs: The generic Creole term for any foreigner, regardless of the colour of their skin. Since the recent United Nations interventions, the African soldiers and experts have also been called blancs.

Boko: A term derived from the Fon word bokomo, which means a vodou priest but which, unlike the houngan, has a negative connotation.

Borlette: From the Spanish borleta. A very popular lottery.

Boule Zin: A ceremony during which a deceased person's spiritual powers are passed on.

Cachiman: A fruit with pips and white flesh.

Chadèque: Grapefruit.

Compas: Traditional urban music from Haiti played in four-four time.

Dambala: A serpent god who is often represented on murals with his spouse Aida Wèdo.

Démunis: The name of a political party. The name literally means The Destitutes.

Erzulie Dantor: An aspect of Erzulie who symbolises endurance and strength, unlike Fréda, who is coquettish.

Erzulie Fréda: A divinity of love, beautiful, coquettish, sensual and extravagant. She is often compared to Aphrodite.

Galipote: A sorcerer, wolf man.

Gayé pay: A fashionable popular dance performed during the carnival.

Gourde: Haitian currency.

Grimelle: A black woman with very light skin and frizzy hair.

Kleren: A first-distillation rum made from sugar cane.

Laloz: A fashionable popular dance performed during the carnival.

Lambi: A marine conch, the flesh of which is valued for its flavour and its alleged aphrodisiac qualities. It is also used as a horn in the peasant community. During the war of independence it was used to call together the insurgents.

Loa: A divinity in the vodou religion, a collection of beliefs and rites of African origin which, closely amalgamated with Catholic practices, form the religion practised by the majority of the rural peasants and urban proletariat in Haiti.

Madame Sarah: The name of a very noisy bird which was initially applied to peasant women who came to sell their wares in town and which is now extended to those who trade between Haiti and the rest of the Caribbean.

Mapou: A sacred tree, home of spirits, with a wide trunk and deep roots, with a similar function to that of the baobab in Africa.

Merengue: Traditional urban music inspired by

Caribbean and Latin American rhythms.

Notre-Dame du Perpétuel Secours: The virgin patron saint of Haiti.

Ogou: A vodou divinity representing fire and combat, a warrior god who is also the blacksmith god in Benin.

Poto-mitan: The central pillar of the vodou peristyle.

Ridden: To be possessed by a vodou spirit, a loa.

Rigoise: A whip made of ox nerves.

Tap-tap: A mode of public transport.

Trese ruban: A dance, inspired by Indian traditions, involving a number of people who hold long ribbons of different colours attached to a central wooden pole and dance around the pole weaving the ribbons as they go.

The quotation on page 102 translates as "The time to talk in signs", a line by the Haitian poet Anthony Phelps.

The Translator

Alison Layland won the Translators' House/Wales Oxfam Cymru 2010 Translation Challenge with a translation of a short story by Yanick Lahens. Having graduated from Cambridge in Anglo-Saxon, Norse and Celtic, Alison Layland is a translator from French, German and Welsh. She is a member of the Institute of Translation and Interpreting, Society of Authors and an Associate of the Welsh Academi.

The Author

Yanick Lahens lives in Haiti. She was born in Port au Prince before moving to France where she was educated at the Sorbonne. Lahens returned to Haiti where she has taught in universities and developed a social contract project. The author of three novels and story collections, her writing focuses on themes such as everyday violence against women, the lives of young people and problems of living in the city.

One of Haiti's most prominent authors, Lahens dedicates a large part of her time to a foundation set up to train young Haitians in sustainable development.

The original French edition of *The Colour of Dawn* won RFO Award, Prix littéraire Richelieu de la Francophonie and Prix Millepages. Yanick Lahens is also the winner of the Leipzig Book Fair Literaturpreis.